# HIGH DIVING

"Everybody hang on," Oz warned as the jet pulled onto the chopper's new heading. "I'm going to try a tree topper." Oz kicked the rudder pedals as he flexed the control column, maintaining their speed as the chopper rotated about its axis. Abruptly the helicopter was flying backward, nose up, facing the oncoming jet.

Aiming the chopper's nose directly toward the F-6, he hit the fire button of his rocket launcher, sending three unguided rockets toward the oncoming Chinese plane.

At nearly the same instant the F-6 pilot fired his cannon; as its muzzle flashed, Oz felt as if he were looking right down its bore. He swung the helicopter through another tree-topper turn, and the projectiles flashed past the chopper, missing the cabin by only three feet. He banked again, racing at right angles from the path of the oncoming jet.

**HarperPaperbacks by
Duncan Long**

Night Stalkers
Grim Reaper
Twilight Justice
Desert Wind
Sea Wolf
Shining Path
Neptune Thunder

DUNCAN LONG *Night* **STALKERS** **BUDDHA'S CROWN**

# HarperPaperbacks
*A Division of* HarperCollins*Publishers*

This is a work of fiction. The characters, incidents, and dialogues are products of the author's imagination and are not to be construed as real. Any resemblance to actual events or persons, living or dead, is entirely coincidental.

HarperPaperbacks    *A Division of* HarperCollins*Publishers*
10 East 53rd Street, New York, N.Y. 10022

Cover illustration by Edwin Herder

First printing: February 1992

Printed in the United States of America

HarperPaperbacks and colophon are trademarks of HarperCollins*Publishers*

10 9 8 7 6 5 4 3 2 1

Pema followed the throngs of people jostling up the narrow, winding street toward the Potala Palace, which towered over the holy city of Lhasa. As he took a deep breath of the cool mountain air, his nostrils were assaulted by the stench of dung, human sweat, and yak leather. The Buddha had said that such smells were more priceless than the scents of the finest perfumes, but Pema was not so sure.

The monk rounded the dusty street corner and passed a row of tiny shops where incense burned; the gray smoke resembled ghostly trails drifting up an invisible mountain. He glanced into one of the storefronts and saw the wizened proprietor hovering anxiously over his woven fabrics, leather goods, and brass candlestick holders.

Pema turned away, shielding his eyes from the bright morning sunlight, and attended to the murmurs of the crowd that surrounded him: "The king of gods has returned," an old ragged woman wheezed to her crony. "The jewel filled with wishes has come to liberate us from the Chinese," a young man exulted to his female companion, urging her on. The rumors wove themselves into a complex tapestry as the monk drifted up the narrow thoroughfare, buoyed by the excited throng.

Like the other three red-robed monks who strode alongside him, Pema knew there actually was a shred of truth in what the crowds were muttering. The new Dalai Lama in his current reincarnation was making militant pronouncements about expelling the unbelievers and restoring the theocracy. Although the operation was cloaked in secrecy, Buddhist monks had been collecting weapons and smuggling them into Tibet, and Pema had even heard whispered rumors that both the Soviets and the Americans were supplying arms.

Yes, the king of the gods was going to expel the Chinese and secure the freedom of his country, but not this day, Pema thought, no matter what the rumormongers said.

The young monk glanced around and recognized that the whole city was surging toward the palace. Everyone sensed that soon the Dalai Lama would again reside in the golden-roofed edifice to rule his people with wisdom and mercy, unlike their cruel Chinese overlords.

"Look," cried the monk next to Pema, grabbing his bare arm and pointing. "The Chinese are blocking the street ahead of us!"

Pema squinted far up the narrow street and discerned the dull green uniforms of the men who were preparing to dam the wave of humanity that approached. The soldiers pointed their spiked bayonets at the crowd, daring the people to continue onward and be impaled on the steel blades that glinted in the sunlight.

*What fools the communists are,* the young

monk thought contemptuously. They exerted their authority merely to show the peasants who was boss; there was no reason for the people to be turned away from the temple today. *Unless they are trying to incite the crowd,* he suddenly realized.

The mass of people noted the presence of the hated soldiers and for a moment seemed to draw back as if to disperse. Then a murmur like rushing water issued from the mouths of the multitude, and abruptly the people surged forward, seeming to dare the Chinese troops to halt them.

Pema tried to stop his forward progress as the crowd behind him shoved on, but he was swept along helplessly with his comrades. As they drew near the soldiers, Pema saw that the troops were being pelted with bits of rock, dung, and even a prayer wheel. The soldiers began to retreat before the furious hail of debris hurled by the multitude.

"It's too soon to attack the Chinese," Pema shouted to his companions, grabbing at the nearest one's elbow in an effort to slow his forward momentum. "The Chinese guards are armed. They aren't going to hold back when—"

"Come on," the other monk yelled, interrupting Pema's diatribe. "We're witnessing the first miracle of the new Dalai Lama. The people are being driven by the gods—see how the Chinese bastards run away? Their guns are useless with this many people. Today we throw the overlords out of Tibet!"

"No! Wait," Pema cried, fighting the rush of people behind him. He battled his way toward a brick wall and tried to keep from being shoved forward but found it impossible. His arms scraped against the rough surface, cutting his skin and making him wince in pain, but he continued moving to keep from being bowled over by the flood of people behind him.

Three feet ahead of him he saw an old woman in a gray shawl stumble and fall, only to be engulfed by the surging body of humanity that flowed over her, unaware of her frantic cries. Pema reached toward her outstretched hand as he passed but was unable to check his forward momentum.

He averted his eyes to keep from seeing the poor woman being trampled. His attention was wrenched away from the tragedy as the first explosive discharge of gunfire echoed down the street. But the mob was deaf; the people continued onward, sweeping Pema along. The monk shivered with fear and concentrated on staying upright in the narrow street.

Suddenly the young Buddhist spied his chance to escape. He half swam through the seething mass of humanity and squeezed into the narrow doorway of an apartment located along the wall.

Catching his breath like a swimmer after a long underwater dive, he plastered himself against the rough wooden door, stepping upward into the portal. As his robe tore and twisted from the crowd jostling past, his fingers strained at the latch, but the entrance was barred. His nails dug into the rusty hasp, and he clung to it, trying to keep from being scraped off his tiny island of safety. One of his sandals was torn off by a passing herdsman who was unaware of what he had brushed against.

Pema heard more gunfire, followed by an unfamiliar thumping. He listened intently, trying to filter out the screams of the crowd as he turned to face

the street, his arms stretched across the door frame
to wedge his body inside its safety.

Abruptly the reverberation increased in volume,
and a black shape hurtled over the street, its shadow
momentarily eclipsing the sun as it passed. The
Tibetans in front of the monk shook their fists at the
passing helicopter and screamed curses that were
lost in the din.

A mist descended from the air in the wake of the
chopper. The cloudlike vapor made Pema shiver as
the cold droplets fell on his skin. The crowd grew
quiet with the passing of the aircraft, and it seemed
to the monk watching them from the doorway that
the momentum of the surging mass slowed.

*Perhaps they are coming to their senses,* Pema
told himself. There was little doubt that their present course would only lead to greater bloodshed
without accomplishing anything.

The monk rubbed his burning eyes and
coughed, inspired perhaps by the sudden hacking of
an old man passing by. Pema cleared his throat and
was aware of how uncomfortable he felt; his chest
and throat felt constricted. He succumbed to the
uncontrollable urge to cough that enveloped him
and found he couldn't stop until he was almost doubled over, his lungs and the muscles in his belly
aching from the fury of his rasp.

The monk straightened up, suddenly aware that
the people around him were stricken in the same
way. With growing terror in their hearts, the crowd
slowed to a halt, many doubled over with coughing
as they struggled to breathe.

Within seconds the people in front of Pema
began to panic. Unable to budge from their tightly

packed positions on the narrow avenue, they tried unsuccessfully to push their way out, their bodies shaking out of control as they struggled to breathe. Many turned blue and lost consciousness, propped up in standing positions by the other choking people who surrounded them.

A woman in front of Pema screamed, her fingernails digging into his face and arms as she struggled to push him out of the doorway in a vain effort to enter the building behind him. Gasping for breath, the monk shoved her back again and again. "No!" he coughed. "It's—" He couldn't even tell her it was locked; the choking sensation in his throat made speech impossible. Finally her eyes rolled up to the top of her eyelids and she passed out, falling into his arms.

Pema's breath rattled in his throat, and he found he was too weak even to cough. His heart pounded in his chest as if it would fracture his ribs. He gazed up and down the street at the corpses standing and kneeling in front of him. Then he toppled forward, his body held upright by the press of bodies.

The densely packed street was filled with crouching purple corpses. Pema stood among them, his lifeless eyes staring toward the Potala Palace as if he were patiently watching for the return of the king of the gods.

# 1

The sky was turning inky to the east of the MH-60K SOA helicopter that flew northward, hugging the muddy Mekong River that carved its way through the no-man's-land between Laos and Burma. Officially the Night Stalkers helicopter didn't exist. Unofficially it was headed into China to knock out a chemical weapons plant that the Chinese had informed the State Department didn't exist. Since it did not officially exist, the Chinese would be unable to protest when the Americans destroyed the facility.

*At least that's the theory,* Captain Jefferson Davis ("Oz") Carson reflected as he strained at the control column to keep the aircraft on its winding course over the river below. The recent use of diphosgene gas by Chinese troops against Tibetan protesters had been the spark that had set Operation Velvet Glove into motion.

The dark clouds to the west of the American chopper silently flashed with lightning, making night appear brighter than day behind the AN/PVS-6 night-vision goggles the pilot wore. Behind the helmet-mounted instrument, his blue eyes scanned the horizon.

"O.T., how are the dogs doing?" the pilot asked his warrant officer, aware that the rough, windy flight had probably made some of the passengers airsick.

"The dogs are okay," reported Lieutenant Harvey "O.T." Litwin, his gruff voice crackling on the intercom as he surveyed the squad of Delta Force troopers sitting in the passenger compartment behind him. The warrant officer rode in the gunner's cabin between Oz and the passenger compartment; O.T. was short for "Old-Timer," since Litwin was the oldest crewman on the MH-60K.

"Better wake up Luger," Oz said. "I think I can hear him snoring again."

"Very funny, sir," SP4 Mike Luger responded over the intercom. The young gunner had the body of a jogger, with muscles so tight that they almost twanged. In contrast to O.T., who sat across from him, Luger was the youngest man aboard—and looked even younger than his twenty years.

The pilot turned to his right. "Death Song, let me know when we're about ten minutes from our SP," he directed. "We'll need to get our gas masks on."

"Will do," the Native American retorted, the eyepieces in his night-vision goggles seeming to flash in the light from the instrument panels.

Oz glanced to the left and saw the dark shape of the weapons pods hanging on the port side of the chopper, suddenly illuminated by the lightning. The MH-60K was equipped with a lethal amount of firepower: dual .30-caliber machine guns, a 70mm Hydra rocket pod, and four Hellfire missiles hung from the struts on either side of the cabin. Adding to the defenses were two door gunners manning .30-caliber GE Miniguns that poked their four barrels from either side of the shadowy aircraft.

Oz hauled the MH-60K into a tight climb over the palm-covered island that jutted out of the river, producing a sense of déjà vu that reminded him of his tours in Vietnam. He leapfrogged the foliage in a giddy jump.

The Night Stalkers helicopter team was part of Task Force Number 160, which had been created from elements of the U.S. Army 158th Aviation Battalion. Based in Fort Bragg, North Carolina, the fliers and the Delta Force squad they carried that night were often called in to do the dirty work when diplomatic channels couldn't cut the mustard. Consequently, the activities of the highly skilled military organization were cloaked in secrecy.

Oz pushed the chopper into another exhilarating dive as they topped a second diminutive island. A gust buffeted the chopper, sending ripples of water undulating across the surface of the river below.

"I've got two radar pingers to the north," Death Song reported, studying the helicopter's cathode ray display in front of him.

"Any chance of them detecting us?" Oz asked.

"Too far away," the navigator answered, glancing at another screen. "Looks like we just entered Chinese airspace."

*The die is cast,* Oz told himself, a surge of adrenaline coursing through his blood. No one spoke for a few minutes as the MH-60K charged on, weaving over the river.

"We're about fifteen clicks from the SP," Death Song announced over the intercom, breaking the silence.

"Get your gas mask on," Oz instructed. "Then

we'll switch from TF/TA to manual." The switch to manual flight would prevent the short-range terrain-following/terrain-avoidance radar from giving them away as they neared their destination in the jungle up ahead. Military intelligence suspected that radar detectors had been planted around the complex to detect outside intrusion from low-flying aircraft.

The pilot waited at the controls while Death Song masked. The navigator removed his helmet and NVG, revealing his tomahawk nose and jet black hair, which was matted with sweat. Within seconds he had his mask in place. "I'll take her now, Captain," he told Oz, his voice muffled by the transponder in the mask.

"You've got the controls," Oz said, releasing the column and the collective pitch lever and removing his helmet. He pulled his gas mask from its carrier on his chest and expertly placed the mask below his chin, thumbs in the straps as he pulled it up over his head. He jerked the straps tight and then placed his hand over the intake valve and inhaled to collapse the rubber and plastic mask, thereby ascertaining that the seal along his face was airtight. Satisfied that it was secure, he donned his helmet and adjusted its mike to the contours of the mask covering his face.

The pilot spoke over the intercom as he lowered his NVG. "All right, I've got the controls." He blinked in the dim light, wishing the gas mask didn't interfere with the smooth fit of the night-vision goggles over his eyes. "I'm taking us off TF/TA now." He held the controls tightly as he disengaged the radar. There was a slight shudder in the vehicle as he made the transition.

"Sudden, have your men got their masks on?" he inquired.

"That's a roger," the Afro-American lieutenant in charge of the squad replied. "We're all masked up."

Oz dropped the chopper slightly to adhere to a nap-of-the-earth flight that held them ten to fifteen feet above the treetops to avoid Chinese radar along the route military intelligence had created for them. He shoved the control column to the left to angle them along a thin beach that cut through the jungle and then pushed the column forward to acquire even more speed. The aircraft raced over the sandy beach, the whooping of its titanium and composite blades echoing off the ebony water and throwing tiny waves in the wake of the downblast.

"There's the SP," Death Song announced, checking the mission control computer on his CRT.

"Arm our weapons," Oz ordered. "Do not, repeat, do *not* fire unless we're attacked."

"Weapons pods armed," Death Song alerted him. "You've got the machine gun pod and 70 millimeters," he added, knowing that the pilot would want to retain control of the gun and the unguided rockets. The copilot/navigator swiveled his NVG upward, where it locked in place over his skull, and then rotated the helmet-mounted display monocle for his Hellfire rockets down, piping an infrared image from the FLIR through his mask into his right eye.

"Both Miniguns are armed and ready," O.T. reported from the gunner's compartment behind Oz, his voice muffled by his gas mask.

"Anything on radar?" Oz asked.

"Still nothing but the two pingers in the distance," Death Song replied.

*So far, so good,* Oz thought, scrutinizing the terrain ahead of him. He shoved down on the collective pitch lever to skim the bank of the river, retaining the radar cover offered by the palm-canopied hill beyond. "That's our ACP, right?" he asked Death Song, studying the hill in front of them.

"That's it," the navigator agreed after double-checking his horizontal situation display screen, where a computer-generated map showed the air control point. "Release point coming up."

"Sudden, we're headed in," Oz announced over the intercom.

"Your dogs are ready," Sudden answered.

The pilot drew back on the control column, decreasing the pitch of the four main blades and slowing their air speed; simultaneously he lowered the collective pitch lever with his left hand, plunging the helicopter toward the small clearing that denoted their LZ.

"I've got radio activity close by," Death Song reported. "Chinese, but I can't tell what they're saying. They sound agitated."

"Better squelch it," Oz ordered.

The copilot flipped a switch on his console, activating the electronic countermeasures pod riding on the side of the chopper. "EW circuits engaged."

The chopper continued its plunge earthward toward the shadowy clearing below. Suddenly, a flash of small-arms muzzles lit the jungle, followed by the clatter of bullets on the exterior of the aircraft.

"LZ's hot," Oz warned over the intercom. "Luger, can you get the snipers along three o'clock?"

"I've got 'em," the gunner answered, yanking his Minigun around and hitting its triggers. The barrels spun and racked the brush, the Minigun's muzzle flashing like lightning.

"I think I saw an APC coming in from the north as we approached," O.T. warned. "Probably about a minute away."

"We'll ignore it for the time being," Oz ordered. "Let's off-load first so our dogs can get into cover."

Oz scrutinized the jungle intensely for several long seconds. Finally O.T. yelled over the intercom: "Our passengers are clear."

"Taking off," Oz warned, yanking the collective pitch lever upward so the chopper leapt into the air. "Let's see if we can find that APC." The pilot skimmed over a palm tree, the landing gear of his chopper brushing aside the leaves as they passed.

"There it is," Death Song said. "At one o'clock."

Oz rocked the chopper to the side, quickly aligning the nose of the MH-60K on the six-wheeled Norinco WZ551 that lumbered down the narrow jungle trail. "I've got it," he said, his finger snaking toward the red button on the control column. He tapped the button three times, and the rocket pod lit up as three Hydra 70 rockets hissed from their tubes.

The 25mm cannon atop the WZ551 swiveled to cover the American chopper and loosed a salvo of shells that sped wide of their target. A moment later the American rocket went wide, creating a fiery blast in the jungle that turned night to day and caused Oz's NVG to shut down momentarily to keep from overloading its circuits. Then the second and third Hydras connected, ripping the APC open like a tin can and throwing shrapnel and debris in all directions. The secondary explosion of the diesel fuel fractured the vehicle and scoured it with flames.

Oz circled the fireball rising from the wreckage;

the aircraft's downblast was whirling the smoke into huge spirals as they passed. Satisfied there was no further danger on the narrow jungle road, he wheeled the aircraft back toward the clearing where they had off-loaded their passengers. Toggling on his radio, the pilot asked the Delta Force commander if his troops needed cover fire.

"Negative on the cover," Sudden's voice crackled over the headphones. "The jungle's hot, but we don't have anybody on our trail—we lost them in the darkness."

"We'll jump ahead, then, and see if we can clear a path for you," Oz said.

"Sounds good," Sudden replied.

"Over and out."

"We've got more ground fire," Luger warned, jabbing on the triggers of his dual-gripped Minigun as they circled the clearing. The fiery tracers from the side door machine gun flashed at the target as hot brass casings spewed from the chute below the weapon.

Oz glanced toward the area Luger had saturated and saw four inert figures lying on the ground. *The Chinese government isn't going to be too happy when they find out about our mission,* he thought glumly, thankful he wasn't a diplomat.

The pilot aligned his chopper onto a new course that would take them to the heavily fortified chemical plant. It was time to get down to serious business.

# 2

Major Chin Ling had been on some odd missions, but he'd never been asked to kidnap a god before. His informant, however, had provided good information in the past; there was no reason to doubt that the Buddha would be exactly where the spy had said he would be.

"We're nearing the temple, Major," the navigator of the Sikorsky S-70 warned Major Ling over the intercom, interrupting the officer's reverie as he piloted the helicopter.

Ling glanced at the dark Tibetan mountainside racing below them, the helicopter almost skimming the icy boulders. "How much farther?" he asked.

"ETA is twelve minutes," the navigator answered in the singsong Chinese spoken by all aboard.

Major Ling switched on his radio to warn the two nearly identical helicopters that trailed him in the night. "Two and Three, we'll go in low as planned; get your troops out and then orbit the lamasery while my grenadiers handle any resistance the monks may offer."

"Acknowledged," the second pilot answered in English.

"Roger," the third replied, the word barely discernible in his broken English.

Ling shook his helmeted head. *"Acknowledged"* *and "roger,"* he thought bitterly. If Chairman Mao had heard words like that from his elite troops, he would have had a screaming coronary.

*Even having a commanding officer with an actual rank would have been unthinkable,* the major added to himself, recalling the attempt of the People's Liberation Army to do away with all badges of rank for fear of elitism. Now they were back to an officer corps similar to that of the West. Mao would have had a fit.

Of course dealings with the West weren't without benefits—as the American chopper Ling flew attested. The helicopter, along with the U.S.-made night-vision equipment and the other gear the major's troops enjoyed, would have been impossible to procure just a few years ago. Mao would be amazed if he could see the Chinese army's equipment these days.

Shoving downward on the collective pitch lever to slice through the frosty air and skim a mountain valley, Ling wondered what the old leader would have thought of their mission. Certainly he would have understood the need to kidnap the young Dalai Lama, who was recognized by the Tibetan Buddhists to be their supreme political and spiritual leader and believed to be the fifteenth reincarnation of Buddha.

The new leader had been schooled in the West and had taken up the fight for Tibetan independence where the late Dalai Lama had left off. Unlike the older man, however, the new leader was encouraging his followers to acquire their freedom through armed rebellion.

That left China in the awkward position of having to crush the Dalai Lama's influence without bringing down the wrath of the West—and precipitating a halt to the flow of high-tech equipment China needed to advance into the twenty-first century. The solution adopted by the Chinese government was to use poison gas on several enclaves of rebels and secretly kidnap the young leader and hold him in an ancient mountain citadel near Saga.

Major Ling was in charge of the kidnapping mission.

Each of the three choppers Ling commanded was heavily armed with twin 12.7x108mm Type 85 heavy machine guns mounted in pods on either side of the fuselage; those guns were controlled by the pilot of the S-70. At either side of the aircraft were grenadiers manning Type W93 belt-fed automatic grenade launchers. The armament had been added to the aircraft by Chinese military engineers who had modified it from its original air-rescue configuration into a combat helicopter.

Ling brought the chopper over the ridge leading to the tantrist monastery, throwing his crew and the ten People's Liberation Army troops behind him into a roller-coaster fall.

"There's the monastery," Ling said, hurling the helicopter into another steep, stomach-wrenching climb over the cliff ahead of them. He leveled out and skimmed the winding path that led to the ancient granite fortress perched on the mountain-top, barely discernible even with the night-vision goggles he wore. "Arm our weapons," he instructed.

"Machine gun pods armed; you have control," the navigator said. "Grenade launchers armed."

"Stand by with the grenade launchers," Ling

ordered over the intercom. "Rake the walls once as we descend and then hold your fire and await my orders after our troops disembark. I don't want to lose any of our men. Signal the troops that we're going in."

The door grenadiers/air crewmen shoved open the side doors of the passenger compartment. The icy wind whipped through the cabin, bringing tears to Ling's eyes as he aligned the nose of the chopper on the wall of the monastery and thumbed the fire button on the control column in his right hand.

Bullets shot from the two machine guns on either side of the chopper, their flames exaggerated by the night-vision goggles. Almost immediately the two grenade launchers joined in the cacophony, belching shells that traveled in long ballistic arcs toward the lamasery; the explosive warheads impacted, rocking the mountain face with their explosions and ripping jagged holes in the ancient walls.

Nearing the central courtyard of the monastery, Ling sighted one of the monks wrapped in a heavy fur coat and brandishing a ceremonial lance as he stared into the gloom, trying to discern the origin of the attack. The major kicked the right rudder pedal and thumbed his machine gun button, sending a stream of projectiles that tore the man to ribbons before he fell to the pavement.

Seeing no other targets, the major dropped the S-70 toward the cobblestones, hovered on the down-blast of the blades, and then expertly set the machine down, bouncing on its hydraulic landing struts.

The soldiers in the passenger compartment leapt to their feet, Type 73 rifles clutched in their cold fingers. Dressed in coarse green uniforms with white snow capes and fur caps with the earflaps strapped under their chins, the soldiers erupted from either side of the aircraft and raced to the living quarters of the monastery.

Ling turned in his seat to be sure the other two choppers had landed without problem and then eyed the walls of the courtyard surrounding them, wondering if the Buddhists had any modern weapons. In a moment the grenadier behind Ling called over the intercom, "All our men are clear."

The major yanked upward on the collective pitch lever, and the S-70 bounded into the air, clearing the way for the next helicopter to come in.

"There's a knot of monks along the wall," the copilot warned. "At three o'clock."

"I see them," Ling answered, his voice cold with contempt as he surveyed their crude bows and arrows. He thumbed the fire button. *Like swatting cold, sluggish flies,* he thought. The flaming salvo dropped the monks in tatters before they could even unleash their pathetic volley of arrows.

The muzzle of a flintlock rifle lit up the spire rising from the wall above them. "Hit the tower at the north of the complex," Ling ordered the grenadiers over the intercom.

The port side grenadier turned his automatic weapon toward the smoky cloud at the peak of the tower, blasting it with a string of thumping discharges. The grenades smashed into the granite spire, ripping holes in it and sending chips of stone gyrating through the darkness. One of the grenades crashed through a narrow window and exploded inside, hurling glass across the courtyard and igniting a blaze inside the library.

"Good," Ling said. "Cease fire so we don't hit our own men on the ground. I don't think these buffoons will pose a threat." He kicked his left rudder pedal and climbed above the other two choppers, which were waiting for their troops to return. As he ascended, he was able to gain a better view of the one-sided battle unfolding in the monastery below. Several of his men were falling, clutching invisible wounds. *The monks have firearms!* "Our men are taking hits from somewhere," Ling informed his crew. "Does anybody see the source?"

"On the right," a grenadier yelled over the intercom. "Along the north wall."

"I've got it," Ling said, spotting the telltale flash from the muzzle of a rifle. He dropped the chopper downward. Apparently his military intelligence briefing hadn't been perfect; several automatic weapons were lighting the night with their staccato discharges, and he could discern the clang of bullets snapping against the underside of his chopper as well.

When the nose of the S-70 was aligned with the flashing muzzle, Ling thumbed the fire button, and the heavy guns on either side of him expelled their deadly fusillade. The tracers arced along the wall, knocking over the gunner below. Ling's second volley ripped into the two gunners concentrating on the Chinese troops in the courtyard.

"More ground fire!" the grenadier yelled over the intercom. "From the far west end of the courtyard. I can take them."

"Do it," Ling ordered.

The grenadier aligned his weapon, took careful

aim through the glowing night sight mounted on it, and mashed the trigger with his finger. Three grenades blooped from the muzzle of the W93 and raced toward their targets. Almost instantly they exploded, sending flames and shrapnel skyward as the men in the center of the blast were torn apart, their weapons thrown from their broken hands.

The radio crackled. "We have our pigeon," cried the voice of Pei Woo, the squad leader.

"Good," Ling answered. "I'm coming in to pick you up. Order the rest of your men back to the choppers before the monks can counterattack."

"Will do."

Ling threw the S-70 toward the courtyard and then centered the control column so his chopper hovered over the clearing for a moment. Satisfied that the area was clear, he lowered the collective pitch lever and aligned his aircraft in the courtyard ahead of the other two Chinese choppers. He quickly lowered the collective pitch lever with his left hand, and the helicopter dropped to the ground, bouncing on its hydraulics and rolling forward a few feet on its tires. Before the helicopter stopped rolling, five soldiers raced out of the darkness to meet it, half carrying between them a figure whose long red robes flapped in the wind.

*So that's God,* Ling chuckled to himself. It seemed impossible that such a scrawny figure could command respect, let alone reverence. Yet the Chinese officer knew that size or looks had little to do with commanding awe or esteem among followers. It must be the one they were after—Woo knew the man by sight from the photos they had obtained of the newest Dalai Lama.

And now the People's Republic of China had the troublemaker. With any luck, Ling would be able to turn the man into a puppet who would do their bidding. *But first we have to get out of the courtyard,* he reflected, noting more muzzle flashes along the wall.

The Chinese soldiers scrambled into the side door and were joined by more of their comrades.

"They're all aboard," shouted one of the grenadiers as he slid the side doors shut.

Ling lifted the S-70 into the air, kicked a rudder pedal to counter the gust that threatened to flatten them against a granite wall, and toggled his radio on. "Two and Three, get out of there as soon as you can."

"Roger. Two is coming up."

Ling raised his helicopter above the courtyard so he could offer suppressing fire if it was needed. As he watched the last of the Chinese troops racing toward the choppers, an explosion of gunfire erupted from the north end of the complex as another of the monks gripping old SKS rifles targeted the Chinese from the parapet. The monks strafed the troops, downing two of them as Ling watched.

The major aligned the nose of his helicopter and unleashed a volley of bullets from his S-70's machine gun pods, bowling over three of the monks with the savage strike and sending the other five scurrying for cover. "Leave your wounded behind," he ordered over the radio, surveying three more flashing muzzles that had sprung up along the opposite wall. "We don't want to give them time to regroup. Get out of the way so Three can take off."

Ling sprayed the wall with gunfire as the second

chopper ascended, leaving the dark forms of the two downed soldiers in the center of the courtyard. The major silently cursed the faulty intelligence briefing that had assured him the monks had only swords and other crude weapons. *Two is clear,* he realized, switching on the radio. "Three, come up," he ordered.

The final chopper wobbled into the air.

"Hit the monastery with another salvo of grenades," Ling ordered his two grenadiers as he took his chopper in behind Three. The grenadiers on either side of the major's helicopter saturated the lamasery with a final salvo of explosive rounds.

"Cease fire," Ling commanded, kicking the right rudder pedal to turn the helicopter about. Then he pushed the control column forward, and they raced away, the underside of the dark helicopter briefly lit by the flames leaping from the burning ruins of the north spire.

The three choppers hurtled through the darkness, the last of the gunfire from the ground spattering off their armor. Ling switched on the radio transmitter and spoke through the mike on his helmet. "Enforcer Home, this is Enforcer One."

"Go ahead, One."

"We have our pigeon. Repeat, we have our pigeon."

"You have the Buddha?" asked the radioman in China, breaking off abruptly when he realized his blunder. "You have the pigeon? Over."

"That is correct," Ling replied through clenched teeth. "You had better be more careful on the radio or I'll personally have your tongue." He paused and then continued. "Over and out."

The major toggled off the radio. *China one, God zero,* he told himself with a smirk; the three S-70 helicopters slashed through the night toward their secret destination.


Twenty-three thousand six hundred miles above Tibet the KH-29 satellite floated in its geosynchronous orbit, drifting weightlessly and processing the radio message it had intercepted from far below. The signal intelligence, or SIGINT, satellite assimilated the message into digital bits and stored it, along with the other babel of signals coming from the broadcasts and electrical noise on the earth below.

An hour passed before the SIGINT dumped the data in its memory into a burst transmitter that relayed the digital bits to a second geosynchronous satellite a quarter of the way around the world. From there the signal bounced earthward to a twenty-foot dish antenna atop a pale blue six-story building affec-tionately dubbed the Big Blue Cube by the Air Force intelligence agents who worked there.

The information from the SIGINT satellite was downloaded into a Cray supercomputer, where it waited for further processing, organizing, and filter-ing by an artificial intelligence program capable of weighing the importance of the communiqués. In the meantime, business went on more or less as usual at the busy satellite control facility on the Onizuka Air Force Base in Sunnyvale, California.

# 3

"We're taking small-arms fire again," Death Song warned.

The American helicopter charged the complex where the secret diphosgene plant was located. The 200-square-meter building looked out of place in the shadowy jungle surrounding it and was ringed with high barbed wire fencing with tall machine gun towers at each corner. Bright floodlights lit the area around the plant while a searchlight stabbed at the nighttime sky.

*It looks like they're expecting company,* Oz thought gloomily.

"Ground fire from the nearest tower," Luger yelled, spotting the stream of flames coming toward the helicopter and then dropping into the jungle behind them.

Oz altered his course slightly and hit the button on his control column to answer the salvo with his own guns, strafing the tower as he approached, hugging the treetops. At the same instant Luger and O.T.'s Miniguns whined explosive blasts from the side doors. The pilot swung them around the complex in a wide tree-topper turn that kept the nose of the MH-60K aligned on the front of the complex.

Oz hit his launch button, and a series of 70mm rockets jumped from their tubes, fins springing into place as they tore away from the chopper and arced downward. They slashed into the tall fence below, blasting chunks of barbed wire away, leaving wide holes in the perimeter that had guarded the complex. The initial blasts were accompanied by secondary explosions inside the grounds of the plant.

"Looks like they've mined the area behind the fence," Death Song remarked, searching the location for any other signs of buried ordnance.

"Yeah." Oz nodded. "I noticed the secondaries." He switched on his radio as the chopper leapt away and hid in the darkness above the plant. "Velvet Glove One to Ground, come in."

"This is Ground One," Sudden's voice replied over the radio. "We're almost in place. You made some nice holes in the perimeter wires for us to come through. Over."

"Do not, repeat, do *not* go in until we can clear a path for you. The area behind the wall is mined."

Sudden swore. "Okay. We'll get into position and wait for your go-ahead. Over and out."

Oz swung around to see six armed men running from inside the complex, Type 68 rifles firing blindly into the night as they tried to hit the helicopter above them. O.T. bathed them with an intense volley; the Chinese soldiers tumbled into a bloody heap.

"I'm picking up more air traffic, coming up fast from the north," Death Song warned, glancing up from his instruments. "Must be at least two jets."

Oz muttered an oath as he booted a pedal and

swung the helicopter to face the rear of the building, where he surmised the generator for the complex had to be located. He launched three 70mm rockets from their pod, sending the missiles into the building, where they exploded. The exterior wall of the structure buckled, throwing the rocket crew coming through the doorway into a heap on the ground. Abruptly the area was plunged into darkness.

"How close are the incoming planes?" Oz called as he swung the chopper around in a half circle and darted over the complex.

"About ten minutes at the most," Death Song answered. "I have all radio traffic suppressed. They must have a ground line out."

"Velvet Glove One, this is Ground," Sudden's voice crackled over Oz's headphones. "We can hear some armor moving in through the jungle. Over."

"We're in the middle of a damned convention," Oz muttered. He toggled on his radio. "Hang on, we're getting into position now. We have company coming in from the air as well, so you aren't going to have long to collect samples and set your charges."

"Just get us through the minefield and we'll be done inside of two minutes."

Oz swung his helicopter around, centering the control column to hover over the perimeter where the fence had been blown clear by his rockets. "Ground One, can you see me?"

"Roger One," Sudden's voice replied. "Lead us in."

Oz shoved the control column forward, nosing the chopper down at the same moment he hit the trigger controlling the machine gun pod. As the MH-60K sped forward, its guns cut a ribbon of earth ahead of them, causing the land mines concealed in

the earth to explode as each was struck by a projectile. The pilot inched the MH-60K forward, ignoring
the clatter of shrapnel and rocks that banged against
the windscreen and underside of the chopper.

Within seconds the explosions stopped, and Oz
lifted his chopper over the complex, swooping
around it in a wide circle. "Ground One, it's all
yours," he radioed the Delta Force troops.

"Thanks, sir," Sudden's voice replied. "Tiptoeing
through minefields is not a piece of cake."

Oz lifted the collective pitch lever in his left
hand, and the helicopter climbed into the dark night.
Below him the American Delta Force soldiers raced
toward the complex, ignoring the crackle of small-
arms fire from Chinese soldiers, who, unequipped
with night-vision gear, shot blindly into the darkness.

The American chopper circled the chemical
weapons plant like an angry hornet, its guns meting out
bursts of gunfire as it located targets of opportunity.

"We've got a bunch of unarmed men headed out
the back," Death Song reported as they circled.
"They look like technicians."

"Let them go," Oz ordered. "We should be gone
before they can get help, and we're not trying to
rack up any body counts here."

Sudden and his men rushed into the building
below the chopper, charging the nearest door that
stood ajar. The soldier on point fired his M16-A3
rifle, expertly putting bursts on either side of the
door and then through it to hit anyone who might
be hidden just inside.

"Fire in the hole!" the soldier next to the point

man yelled, tossing a percussion grenade into the building.

The soldiers crouched as the stun grenade exploded, its bright light casting shadows in the darkness. The five troopers closest to the entrance rushed into the building, leaping over the corpse in the doorway, their rifles blazing.

Sudden spun around and flashed a hand signal, ordering the remaining men to spread out along the unlit building. The soldiers shifted positions almost soundlessly, rifles held at the ready as their NVGs pierced the darkness around them.

"All clear!" a soldier called from the door.

Sudden turned and rushed for the doorway, blinking behind the gas mask for a moment, intensely aware of the narrow field of vision his NVG offered. He looked around inside the building, which was crammed full of large tanks and pipes. "Where's Frank?" he demanded.

"Here, sir," one of the masked soldiers hollered, approaching the lieutenant at a trot.

"Got your samples?"

"Just about, sir. I need to check one more vat down there."

"Hurry up."

"Yes, sir," the soldier replied, scampering down a walkway.

"Savage?" Sudden called.

"Here, sir. Our explosives are in place. A couple of the canisters seem to be leaking. Some of the stray bullets may have punctured them."

"Great!" Sudden exclaimed. "Let's hurry up and get out of here."

"Yes, sir."

The lieutenant watched as his men completed their tasks. The officer suddenly felt claustrophobic inside the hot rubber gas mask. *I'm going to be real glad when this shit's over,* he told himself.

Minutes later Sudden's voice crackled over Oz's headset. "We've got our samples, and we're ready for dust-off. I've got one casualty—looks like a leaky mask. There's definitely some type of poison gas in here. One of the canisters is leaking from stray hits— looks like eight or nine of our friends got wasted by their own gas."

"We're coming in for you now," Oz replied. "You need to really move it; our incoming company is almost here. Over."

"That's a roger, One. I think we've worn out our welcome down here anyway."

Within seconds, Oz had landed and the Delta Force troops were racing for the helicopter, ducking their heads as they came.

"Enemy troops in the brush to the east," O.T. advised via the intercom as the din of his Minigun echoed off the face of the building. The shooting abruptly stopped following the Minigun burst, and the night was silent except for the thumping of the helicopter's blades and engine.

"Everyone's on board," Luger yelled.

Oz lifted the collective pitch lever, and they leapt into the air. He quickly shoved on the control column and launched a salvo of rockets into the jungle where he'd seen the backblast of a rocket. The unguided RPG sped past as his Hydras exploded in the foliage.

"More enemy troops approaching to the south," Luger warned. "Looks like they have a tank with them."

"Cease fire—ignore them," Oz yelled as he swung the chopper around to face into the wind. He shoved the control column forward as he lifted the collective pitch lever for maximum ascent. The MH-60K rapidly climbed and melted into the darkness, becoming lost from sight to those on the ground.

"We definitely have two jets overtaking us," Death Song cautioned. "ETA in thirty seconds. One of 'em's pinging us."

Oz lowered the collective pitch lever to take them closer to the ground. *If I can just reach the valley ahead,* he told himself.

Death Song glanced toward the pilot. "They've got to have us. They're altering course to follow us."

"Have to shake them, then," Oz said. "Stand by on the Hellfire in case we have to face off. Hang on, everybody, I'm breaking ninety." The pilot shoved the control column to the side and kicked his left rudder pedal, turning them into a steep roll that was so dangerous that the Army had banned the manuever. But Oz knew it was his only chance to lose the oncoming jets.

The MH-60K cruised over the edge of the hill ahead of them, then dropped groundward. The pilot brought the aircraft out of its roll and pinned his passengers to the side with the *g* forces created as he leveled out. He throttled the overextended machine to its maximum speed of 296 kilometers per hour and raced down the hillside.

"They're altering course to cut us off," Death Song warned. A moment later he added: "The first one's overshot us. Must have lost us in the ground clutter. The second one still seems to have us."

Oz shoved the collective pitch lever down even more, and the chopper dropped like a rock, plunging toward the dark earth below. The pilot fought the controls, narrowly missing a palm tree as they tore through the foliage ahead of them, tail and main rotors severing the thin branches.

The pilot bit his lip, hoping he wouldn't lose control of the chopper as he lifted the collective pitch lever and bounced the aircraft in the tiny clearing, the ground effect air pushing upward from the earth. Despite the noise of the MH-60K's engines, the air thundered as the MiG-21 passed overhead.

"Think he spotted us?" Oz asked, setting the helicopter onto the ground and looking upward. But he failed to see the plane that had passed over.

"He's slowing to circle," Death Song replied. "And the first one's coming back to help. Hang on."

The American pilot grasped the collective pitch lever in his left hand, ready to take off at a moment's notice if necessary. He studied the silhouettes of the trees around him and wondered if the jet pilots would miss seeing the American chopper on their second pass of the unlit jungle.

"Here they come," Death Song warned.

In the distance, the low roar of the jets signaled their approach.

"They're almost on top of us," Death Song cautioned as the tumult of their engines grew closer.

# 4

Major Ling pulled the heavy fur cape around himself and cursed the cold, his boots echoing in the granite hall. The room looked impressive with its granite walls, but it was also impossible to heat. He set his flight helmet on the crude table in front of him and settled his heavy frame into the padded chair behind. Stroking his long mustache, brittle after his passage through the icy wind, he surveyed the old monastery the Chinese government had commandeered for their operations.

*This is nothing like the warmth of my home in Macao,* he reflected. Would he ever see China again? Gassing peasants and kidnapping religious fanatics—his world had gone mad. A fifty-year-old military commander known both for his skill as a military strategist and for his harsh treatment of those who didn't follow the party line, Ling had been instrumental in the Chinese purges of intellectuals during Mao's reign.

But all that had ended with the violence of Tiananmen Square; while the government had won the battle, it had lost the war. The West had exerted pressure on the government to either change or risk the loss of the goods and equipment needed to bring the Chinese out of their poverty and Third World status into a major industrial force. With the behind-the-scenes changes forced on them by the West, Ling had found himself all but exiled to Tibet as newer, more flexible leaders took over control of China.

*But now those young hotshots need my expertise here in what the locals like to call "the roof of the world,"* Ling thought scornfully. And they'd given him the men and equipment to do the job.

The sound of boots tramping toward him interrupted his thoughts. He turned slowly to find Lieutenant Woo standing stiffly at attention in front of him.

"Is the prisoner secure?" Ling asked the officer.

"Yes, Major. But . . ." His voice trailed off as if he had suddenly lost the ability to speak.

"What?"

"Nothing, sir."

"Tell me."

"Some of the men are—frightened."

"Of what? The monks have no way to attack us here."

"No, sir, not the monks. The prisoner."

"That silly little scarecrow of a man we captured tonight?"

"Yes, sir."

Ling shook his head. Chinese peasants, that was what most of his men still were. They believed in herbs and hexes and magic. *I'll change some of that in the next few days,* he vowed to himself. "He's secure in his cell, isn't he?"

"Yes, sir."

"That's all that matters. He's not going to melt

into the walls or strike the guards blind."

"No, sir," Woo nodded, smiling with embarrassment at the foolishness of his men's fears. In the presence of the major, his own fears lost their former potency.

"Now see if you can get some heat into this damned tomb of a building," Ling ordered, sitting back in his chair and seeming to dismiss the officer completely from his thoughts as he rubbed the bald spot at the top of his head.

Jim Chung sat in his office at the CIA headquarters in Langley, Virginia, waiting for the Sun Microsystem workstation in front of him to come on line. Though it took only seconds, it seemed to the computer expert that it took a lifetime for it to check for line integrity, exchange code words with the computers at the other end, and then pull back into its program. And while in theory a user could do other things on the workstation while waiting for all the electronic handshaking to get finished, in fact he didn't have any other work to do.

He leaned back in his office chair and puffed nervously at his pipe, scratching at a slanted eyelid that betrayed his Oriental heritage. He rubbed the scar over the eye, the badge he carried from Vietnam, and remembered his own one-on-one brush with communism when his family had fled Vietnam after the American pullout. He thought of the recent chemical attacks the Chinese had inflicted on innocent Tibetan civilians. *Different times and places but the same old brutality,* he told himself. He was glad to be in a position to help this time.

Finally the computer beeped, and his thoughts returned to the task at hand. Tossing the extinguished match that had relit his pipe into the ashtray, he leaned his wiry frame forward and engaged the computer.

With quick precision, his lean fingers tapped the keys, transporting him through the menu-driven maze at the other end of the line at the satellite control facility at the Onizuka Air Force Base in Sunnyvale, California. Within a minute he was in the search mode of the giant California computer, sifting through the data bases collected from spy satellites around the globe. He picked out the appropriate data dump and hit the third selection on the screen to secure access to it.

KEY WORDS? the computer prompted in large white letters on the blue workstation screen.

Chung checked the printout from the State Department and then entered the words the computer program would search for, sifting through its raw data. "Dalai Lama, Tibet, kidnap," he typed. There was no doubt in his mind about the nature of the information the State Department wanted; the newspapers had been full of sketchy details of the Dalai Lama's return and the use of poison gas to crush the Tibetan attempt to push the Chinese out. Now voices in the Congress were calling for the President to put pressure on the Chinese.

SECONDARY WORDS? the computer demanded silently.

The CIA agent thought a moment, then lifted the phone and punched in a number.

"Reference library," a female voice at the other end answered.

"Mary, this is Chung," the agent said. He spoke to her briefly, then waited impatiently for three minutes as she checked her files for more information. Finally she found what he needed; the information passed directly from the computer in the library to his workstation.

"It arrived without any problem," Chung told the librarian, checking his screen. Thanks." He set the phone back onto its cradle and carefully sent the three words on the screen into the menu window of his program.

Another tap on the keyboard erased the library menu, leaving behind "Buddha, Reincarnation, God." He studied the three words for a moment and then hit the return key.

LANGUAGES(S)?

"Chinese, Tibetan, English," Chung typed.

SEARCHING, the computer screen flashed. He pushed his chair away from the console and puffed at his pipe, only to discover that it had gone out again. *Time for a break,* he thought, tapping the cherry-scented tobacco from his pipe into the ashtray. He checked his watch and then rose from the workstation. Computer searches often took up to an hour, and he didn't have anything to do other than wait around. If he hurried, he could still grab a sandwich at the canteen before it closed.

Oz listened intently as the first jet roared overhead. A moment later the second passed, rocking the jungle in its wake.

"Either jet slowing?" the pilot asked, crouching tensely at the controls of the MH-60K.

"Negative," Death Song replied. "They're both circling east. Looks like they think we're headed back the same way we came in."

"They lost us!" Luger yelped over the intercom, unable to contain his relief.

"Great," Oz said, releasing his breath. "Let's let them put some distance between us and then let's get out of here."

"Roger that." Death Song nodded, watching the radar on his screen as the planes vanished into the distance.

Within an hour Oz had left Laotian airspace and entered Thailand. "Looks like we made it," he informed his crew. "Death Song, better uplink to the COMSAT so we can let Commander Warner know the mission is accomplished," he added. *There should be a few sighs of relief in Washington,* the pilot thought to himself.

Death Song activated the radio that linked the helicopter's communications system to the satellite in space high above them. Once the computers in the satellite and helicopter had exchanged access codes and established a line to Fort Bragg, Oz briefly outlined the success of the mission to Commander Warner.

"And you have your one casualty stabilized?" the commander asked after Oz had finished.

"Yes, sir. The medic says he experienced only a mild exposure to the gas from a leak in his mask. Codeine got his cough under control, and the bottled oxygen we had on board seems to have brought him around."

"He'll be all right?"

"Yes, sir. But I suspect he'll be out of it for a while."

"I'll have medical personnel standing by when you get back to friendly territory."

"I guess we'll be back home in bed by this time tomorrow," the helicopter pilot said.

"I'm afraid it's a negative on that," Warner replied, his voice altered to a metallic tone by the distance and distortion of the radio wave as it traveled through the atmosphere. "I'm not sure what's up, but you're to sit tight when you reach your base. I'll get your new orders to you as soon as I receive them. In the meantime, check out a paper—I think you'll find some of the headlines interesting. And you and your crew better get as much rest as you can. Looks like you might have a tough one coming up. That's all I can tell you right now. Over."

"Some of these guys look like they could use some serious rest, sir, so we'll be taking your advice," Oz replied. "Over and out." The pilot toggled off the radio, wondering just what type of mission they'd be performing next.

Jim Chung's sneakers squeaked on the polished floor of the hallway as he headed for CIA Director Harold Maxwell's office, acutely aware of his crumpled suit jacket and the tuna stain on his silk tie. He'd heard that some bigwig was with the chief, and he had little reason to doubt the rumor, for what Chung had discovered had momentous ramifications.

"Good morning," Maxwell's secretary greeted him as he strode into the office, avoiding the eyes of the President of the United States, who stared at him from the painting on the wall. "Mr. Maxwell said to go on in when you finally got here."

Chung tried not to wince and drew himself up, making himself as erect as his five-foot frame would allow. Squaring his shoulders, he marched toward the doorway that led into the inner sanctum of Maxwell's conference room.

"Here he is now," Maxwell announced as the agent entered the conference room. To his surprise, Chung noticed for the first time how much the director looked like a smiling Buddha. *Too much time at your computer,* the agent told himself, trying not to shake his head or otherwise betray his thoughts.

Maxwell sat at the head of a long walnut table that almost filled the room. A row of computer monitors, one for each of the twenty chairs around the table, was nestled into its top.

"Good morning, Agent Chung." Maxwell smiled plastically, waving Chung toward the chair next to him. "Mr. Chung is our computer whiz and expert on the Tibetan situation," the director explained. "Chung, do you know Secretary of State Mark Taylor?"

"Uh, no, sir," Chung stammered, shaking the hand of the weasel-faced man in the gray pin-striped suit; the secretary of state's iron handshake threatened to break his fingers. The agent muttered a "glad to meet you" and searched for his chair, thankful there were no more hands to shake.

"Show Mr. Taylor what you've found," Maxwell said.

Chung sat down, centered the computer keyboard in front of him, and punched up the code that connected the instrument to the workstation in his office.

"Harold tells me you have some intercepts of interest," the secretary of state remarked, glancing at his watch.

"Yes, sir," Chung replied, licking his lips. The computer screens flickered, throwing light across the ceiling like artificial lightning. "Here they are now, sir."

Taylor checked the monitor in front of him, noting the large number of asterisks that designated words the satellite wasn't able to intercept:

"*** HOME THIS *** ENFORCER ONE."
"GO ***, ***."
"WE *** *** PIGEON. REPEAT, *** HAVE OUR
PIGEON."
"YOU HAVE *** BUDDHA?" [Pause] "YOU ****
THE PIGEON? OVER."
"THAT *** CORRECT. *** BE *** CAREFUL *** ***
RADIO OR I'LL PERSONALLY *** *** ***. *** AND
OUT."

"'Buddha' is the key word here," Taylor said,
tapping his screen.
"Right," Chung agreed. "That's how I located
this message by searching through the latest data
dumps. I then took the liberty of studying the actual
digital recording—"
"Chung speaks fluent Chinese and Tibetan,"
Maxwell interrupted, leaning toward Taylor.
"I studied the recordings and was able to piece
together a few more words to get this translation
from the original Chinese," Chung continued, tapping another key.

"ENFORCER HOME THIS *** ENFORCER ONE."
"GO AHEAD, ***."
"WE HAVE *** PIGEON. REPEAT, WE HAVE OUR
PIGEON."
"YOU HAVE *** BUDDHA?" [Pause] "YOU HAVE
THE PIGEON? OVER."
"THAT *** CORRECT. *** BE MORE CAREFUL ***
*** RADIO OR I'LL PERSONALLY *** *** ***. OVER
AND OUT."

"Parts of the message were repeated," Chung explained. "By inserting these and making several other assumptions about what was said, we end up with this." He hit a third key, and more words appeared, replacing several of the lines of asterisks. "This is the best we can do."

Taylor studied the transcript that appeared on his screen.

"ENFORCER HOME, THIS IS ENFORCER ONE."
"GO AHEAD, ONE."
"WE HAVE OUR PIGEON. REPEAT, WE HAVE OUR PIGEON."
"YOU HAVE *** BUDDHA?" [Pause] "YOU HAVE THE PIGEON? OVER."
"THAT *** CORRECT. *** BE MORE CAREFUL *** *** RADIO OR I'LL PERSONALLY *** *** ***. OVER AND OUT."

"They said, 'You have the something Buddha'?" Taylor read from the screen. "It's hard to believe that would mean anything other than that they have the Dalai Lama, just as our source inside China indicated. This seems to confirm that."

"Exactly," Maxwell agreed. "Unless they've taken to stealing religious artifacts," he snickered, "in which case this is a wild-goose chase."

"Do you know the exact point where this message originated?" Taylor asked Chung. "Harold said something about that earlier."

"Yes, sir," the agent answered. "I've been monitoring an area of intense activity near Saga for several weeks now. I'm betting that's where the Dalai Lama is being held—if they really have him. The same voice, which we believe is Major Chin Ling—"

"I gave you a copy of his file, Mr. Secretary," Maxwell interrupted.

"We believe that's Ling on the transmission," Chung continued. "He often sends coded messages to China. Most of what we've deciphered suggests that he's setting up a base in one of the old monasteries the Chinese forced the Buddhist monks to leave following their Cultural Revolution in Tibet during the 1960s."

As Taylor tugged at his lower lip, Chung waited nervously, listening to the hum of the monitors in the room. He knew that with the breakup of the Warsaw Pact and the deterioration of the governments in India and Russia, the administration saw a need to keep China from becoming too strong. One way to do that would be to have a free Tibet to act as a buffer zone in the region.

Taylor finally spoke. "President Crane needs to know if the Dalai Lama is still alive and, if the Chinese have him, where he's hidden."

"Since this message confirms what our other sources have suggested," Maxwell began, scratching his potbelly, "I'd say we're going to need a man in Tibet to check out Major Ling."

"Right," Taylor agreed. "We need to know if the Dalai Lama's still alive and, if he's been captured, free him and put him back into the game. How soon can you get into the region to check all this out?"

"The best Night Stalker team we have is in the area," Maxwell answered immediately. "I've requested that they be kept on standby on the USS *America* when they return from their previous mission. The ship and its task force are in the Bay of

Bengal off India right now, just a short hop from the area where the transmission originated."

"What kind of time frame are we looking at?" Taylor asked.

"I could have someone to the aircraft carrier in about twelve hours if we hustle. The Night Stalkers could have my man in Tibet within another few hours."

"Sounds good," Taylor agreed. "We need that information ASAP. And we'll have to act quickly since we don't know whether the Chinese are planning to keep the Dalai Lama alive. So the sooner we act, the better. We want to keep everything as covert as possible."

"I understand." Maxwell nodded. "How about moving some more Night Stalkers choppers and Delta Force troops to the ship so they'll be ready if we need to extract the Dalai Lama."

"I'll relay your request to the President," Taylor said. "President Crane wants to give heavy encouragement to the Tibetan rebels, and although this needs to remain covert, the President doesn't want this to turn into another Kurdish situation. We need to keep a strong leader in place whom the people will follow and then give him massive covert support. With any luck, Tibet will regain its independence."

"Then it's a go?" Maxwell asked.

"Right," the secretary of state agreed, standing up and checking his watch again. "If you'll excuse me, gentlemen, I have another appointment. But I'll get things moving on positioning the rest of the operation's personnel on the USS *America* in case we need to act in a hurry."

After shaking hands with the two men, Taylor strode out of the room, briefcase in hand.

"Who will you be sending in, sir?" Chung inquired after the door had closed.

Maxwell flashed him another plastic grin. "I'd figured you'd have guessed that by now, Chung. You're the special agent in charge of Tibetan affairs."

"But—"

"You've got all the qualifications. And most of our agents are 'big white guys' that'd stick out like sore thumbs in Tibet. You speak the language fluently, know the people, and understand the customs. You're in excellent physical shape, and you know what we're looking for."

"But—"

"I will accept no arguments," Maxwell insisted, raising his hand to prevent the agent from protesting. "Can you be ready to board a plane in fifteen minutes?"

Chung thought a moment, his mind reeling. "How about half an hour?" he requested. "I've had my bug-out bag packed since I came to work here ten years ago, but I'm not sure—"

"Half an hour, then," Maxwell interrupted. "Pick up a new transmitter. And you'll need a pistol—better pick up a clean one, since you may have to toss it."

"Which plane?"

"I'll have our helicopter ferry you to the nearest jet we can line up—probably a military transport. I'll handle that. I'll have my secretary get the info to you as soon as we know."

"Yes, sir," Chung said, realizing he had no recourse but to go along with the flood of events that threatened to engulf him.

"And good luck," Maxwell added, shaking the startled agent's hand. "I wouldn't be sending you in if you weren't qualified. Relax—it'll be a piece of cake. Quick in, find out if they have the Dalai Lama in that stronghold, then radio for the Night Stalkers to come pick you up. Then you'll be home free. Those Army jocks are slick at sneaking in and out of enemy territory." He stood up and ushered Chung to the door. "Any questions?"

"Uh, no, sir. I should be able to get appropriate clothing from our in-house shop. I guess that about takes care of everything."

"Don't forget the Kaopectate."

"Already in the bug-out bag." Chung grinned.

"Better get a move on, then," Maxwell said, his face softening for a moment as he shook the agent's hand.

"Yes, sir," Chung said. He turned and closed the door behind himself. As he stood in the outer office for several seconds, the events of the last several minutes sank into his consciousness.

"Did you need anything else?" the secretary asked.

"No," Chung answered, his voice resolute. "Nothing I can't handle. I'll be in either my office or the house shop when you have the plane reservation info for me."

"I'll contact you there," she answered.

Chung glanced at the wall where the President's countenance smiled down at him, grinned back, then hurried into the hallway, his sneakers squeaking on the polished floor as he sprinted toward his office.

# 6

"This is NS-1 calling CV-66," Oz radioed to the USS *America,* which was bobbing on the horizon south of them.

The radio sputtered noisily, then cleared as the channel became occupied with a carrier wave. "NS-1, we read you loud and clear. Go ahead."

"NS-1 requests permission to land. Over," Oz called.

"NS-1, you are cleared to come on in. Our eye in the sky has you on radar. Continue on your current heading and maintain your altitude. Use the aft helideck area for landing as usual. We'll keep your space warm and put a light in the window. Over."

"Thank you, CV-66," Oz replied. "Over and out."

Within minutes the U.S. Army chopper had passed through the invisible web of radar that surrounded the USS *America,* along with the ships, boats, and planes in its task force, and rushed toward the four-acre flight deck of the Kitty Hawk-class aircraft carrier. The ship rolled below Oz's chopper as he approached the helideck at the aft end.

The battleship gray of the conning tower

appeared pink in the sun, which seemed to rise from the sea as a fog of burnt diesel fuel climbed into the still air above the carrier. The ship stretched 1,046 feet in length as its four turboshaft engines propelled the vessel forward through an ocean that retained the blackness of the night in its murky depths.

Far in the distance, nearly lost in the haze of the watery horizon, sailed the other members of the carrier group. The cruisers and antisubmarine warfare escort ships surrounding the USS *America* provided an interlocking screen of electronic eyes and ears as well as antiair and antisubmarine defenses that were integrated into the complex routes patrolled by the aircraft the carrier kept in the sky.

The MH-60K descended toward a deck that was a mass of activity, which the multihued deck crews busy with their tasks, lugging fuel lines, guiding planes on and off lifts, and relaying signals to the pilots of incoming and outgoing jets. A row of seven A-6 Intruders sat on the deck, wings folded upward like giant insects, while eight F-14A Tomcats stood frozen on the opposite edge, canopies open to enable their pilots to prepare rapidly for takeoff if an emergency arose.

Oz settled his MH-60K onto the flattop as a Tomcat streaked forward on a powerful steam catapult. The device hurled the plane down the diagonal airstrip and off the edge of the ship, where its jet engines noisily brought it to full speed to climb skyward.

Oz rapidly slammed the collective pitch lever down as his chopper alighted on the deck, anchoring the wheels to the swaying surface as he cut the engines' throttles and applied the brakes. Then he and Death Song went through the procedure required to shut down the chopper's systems and secure it while deck crewmen placed chocks and chains around the MH-60K's three wheels to prevent it from rolling if its brakes failed. Suddenly, the side doors of the Army helicopter slid open and tired Delta Force troops spilled onto the gyrating deck.

"Our dogs are out and all loose gear stowed," O.T. informed Oz over the intercom a few minutes later. "Couple of the Delta troops were so stiff, they fell down when they got out—these Navy wags will never let them live that down."

"I don't doubt it." Oz chuckled. "When we disembark, we better go slow and get our sea legs or we'll be the butt of their ribbing." The pilot turned toward his copilot. "How's it look, Death Song?"

"Shut down and no problems," the Native American replied.

"Then let's see if we can find some hot chow and some nice soft bunks," Oz said.

"In that order," O.T. agreed from the back.

As the four Army airmen gingerly climbed out of the chopper, a Navy ensign came sprinting across the deck toward them, sidestepping through the maze of crewmen and equipment.

"Here comes trouble," O.T. predicted. "Ten to one he's got a new assignment for us. I've seen that look in their eyes before."

The other three airmen didn't take him up on the bet.

The Dalai Lama inspected his bleak surroundings in the dim light that filtered through iron bars on the door. The cell was tiny: two meters by six meters, with straw in the corner for a bed—or perhaps a latrine, judging from the smell.

*The poor Chinese. They think they can imprison me with mere walls of stone,* he reflected. He closed his eyes, and his fingers searched each crevice between the cold blocks of the granite wall; the surface became a huge maze that expanded as he explored. His shivering stopped, and he felt warm.

The *bodhisattva* was free again.

He stared upward at Mount Kailas. The rounded holy mountain that so often depicted the "snow jewel" in both Hindu and Buddhist art towered above him, its peak capped with snow, sparkling white in the sunshine. Mists rose from the valleys and condensed into tiny flecks of ice as they reached the pinnacle to descend in tumbling miniature rainbows of angel dust.

The Dalai Lama, king of the gods, watched a moment, then hurtled through space, twisting and dodging between the tiny flakes of glittering ice. Finally he tired of his joyous flight and returned to earth.

As he settled onto the ground, he turned to study one of his followers, who was pursuing his sacred pilgrimage up Mount Kailas. The pilgrim circled the crest of the mountain in his two-day, thirty-mile journey, pausing to lift his praise at the *chorten,* an altar of prayer flags that waved on their ropes in a multitude of tattered colors. Once around the holy Mount Kailas, the center of the universe, and the pilgrim would have his sins washed away. If he circled the mountain 108 times—a feat few achieved—he would experience nirvana in his lifetime.

The buddha smiled, then extended his hand to bless the ragged beggar. The man smiled back, seeming to sense the object of his adoration close by, even though the *bodhisattva* was invisible to him.

"Continue on your journey, for it is blessed," the Dalai Lama told him. Then he turned and leapt into the air, flying like a bird down the hillside. He slowed and circled the five pilgrims who rested on the ridge, eating *sampa*—cold, parched grain meal that they ate with their fingers—and drinking butter tea—traditional foods of the faithful.

The sound of screaming distracted the Dalai Lama's concentration; the scene around him dimmed and became transparent, the black walls of his prison intruding into the ghostly image.

"The Buddha is gone!" the voice cried again in Chinese. "The cell is empty. The Buddha is gone!"

The *bodhisattva* opened his eyes and was back in his cell, his hand still touching the cold wall. A bright flashlight was shoved through the bars in the doorway, and the Dalai Lama blinked at the bright beam that searched his face.

"You're crazy," yelled a voice the Buddha recognized as belonging to Lieutenant Woo. The flashlight was jerked back into the hallway and switched off, plunging the cell into darkness. "He's right there," Woo explained. "Now quit acting like a stupid old woman."

"But the cell was empty," the guard protested. "I unlocked it and walked in. It was empty! No one was—"

"Nonsense," Woo interrupted. "You fell asleep again and dreamed it all. Now shut up before you wake everyone in the citadel. And if you fall asleep once more, you'll be in the cell next to this religious fraud."

"Yes, sir."

The officer's heels tramped down the hallway, leaving the guard with his thoughts.

Inside the cell the *bodhisattva* smiled. A moment later the guard peeped through the bars and flashed his light at the monk, assuring himself that the Dalai Lama was still safely detained inside the cubicle.

"I'm still here for now," the Buddha said, and the light snapped off. *The Chinese will never be able to keep me here.* He smiled to himself. Even if they killed him, he would simply be reincarnated in another body to lead his country to independence.

But it wouldn't come to that—he was certain. Already his spirit was free to roam where he willed it. And he could sense that his followers were, this very moment, meeting to create a plan to free him.

He closed his eyes. *They need my guidance.* He would travel in his thoughts to sit in on their meeting, perhaps counseling them as they formed their plans. Certainly he could show them exactly where he was inside the citadel. That would speed their efforts and make the rescue less dangerous for them to carry out.

*The Chinese are lost,* the *bodhisattva* thought as he closed his eyes to attempt his mind travel through space. The communists fought with flesh and iron; he fought from the higher ground of the gods.

The night was brightly lit by his night-vision goggles as Oz piloted the MH-60K at thirty feet, his nap-of-the-earth flight preventing the aircraft from being detected by civilian or military radar as he neared the shores of Bangladesh. Once over land, the pilot would follow the Padma and Meghna rivers northward, turn west, then head north again, negotiating the Gangtok pass to penetrate the lower parts of the Himalayan mountain range and enter Tibet.

The pilot's mind wandered to the strange passenger they had taken on board. "Agent Chung," the pilot had said, shaking the Oriental's hand and eyeing the odd Tibetan garb the man wore.

"You're not the one they call Oz, are you?" Chung asked.

"I'm afraid so," Oz admitted, a tired expression on his face.

"Wow. I've finally met you," the young agent enthused. "I've heard a lot of tales about your flying."

"We'll be taking off in about fifteen minutes," Oz said modestly, a slight blush creeping up the back of his neck as he tried to change the subject.

"I'll be ready by then," Chung promised, pulling a wood rasp out of his pocket. He sat down on the metal chair in the center of the tiny cabin he'd been assigned on the USS *America* and proceeded to skin up the toes of the yakhide boots he wore with the jagged teeth of the rasp.

Glancing up and noting the pilot's quizzical expression, the agent smiled and proceeded to explain. "The CIA makes brand-new clothing for its agents to wear on missions. Unfortunately, nobody in Tibet has much of anything that's brand new. If I appeared in this outfit the way it was issued, I'd find myself in a Chinese prison in short order." He noticed that Oz seemed anxious to leave. "I'll see you in fifteen minutes, then," he finished.

"We need to alter our course to the left four degrees," Death Song said, transporting the pilot's thoughts back to the present. The navigator tapped the gyromagnetic compass as if to emphasize his message.

"Left four degrees," Oz answered, kicking his left rudder pedal and watching the horizontal situation display screen as he adjusted their course. As he straightened out the MH-60K, he glanced through the chin window to see the sea hurtling past, indicating their speed. Through the dome window above, he noticed the stars twinkling brightly, seeming to race along with the aircraft.

"How's our dog, O.T.?" Oz asked over the intercom.

There was a pause as the warrant officer glanced back into the crew compartment. "Sleeping like a baby, feet propped up and head sprawled over that leather backpack he's carrying. You think he knows what he's doing? He looks about as young as Luger."

"Funny," the other gunner's voice piped in. "You are the only guys I know who think getting old is some kind of virtue."

Chung reposed in the passenger compartment, eyes closed as if he'd been lulled to sleep by the deafening drone of the MH-60K's twin engines. In fact, he was wide awake, too nervous to sleep.

The agent carried a Heckler & Koch P-7-M13 pistol, along with a spare magazine for it, concealed in his heavy yakwool coat. The pistol was loaded with 9mm fragmenting Mag-Safe cartridges to stop opponents quickly if he was forced to use it. Hidden in his left boot was a hypodermic syringe kit with a vial of sodium pentothal; it could be utilized to help loosen a soldier's tongue if the need arose. In his other boot was a small SOG Toolclip that could be unfolded for use as a file, knife, screwdriver, or pliers.

On his belt hung a wooden-handled knife in a leather sheath; beside it was a flint for making fires. Both were often seen on the belts of guides, yak herders, and other nomadic people—known as *drokpa* in Tibetan. He hoped this cover would satisfy casual questions if he was forced to explain his reasons for wandering about the area to the Chinese authorities.

Taped to the agent's right thigh under his baggy pants was the transmitter with which he'd make contact with an overhead COMSAT when it was time for the Night Stalkers to pick him up. Chung hoped to get the transmitter into action in no time flat. While he was excited about his chance to see

Tibet again, the dangers involved eliminated any possible joy for him; he would be glad to return to American soil in one piece.

*Quick in and quick out,* the agent promised himself. Then he was going to take that vacation he'd been putting off. The CIA could get along just fine without him—who was he kidding about putting off his vacation? And he'd more than earned it this time. Maybe a nice trip to the Bahamas. Yeah, that sounded really good.

The monks were aware that the secret meeting was dangerous; after killing nearly two million Tibetans since the communist takeover in 1949, the Chinese wouldn't think anything of adding twenty more Buddhist clergymen to the long list of the dead.

"I feel *his* presence here," Targye told the others as they sat in the darkened mud-brick room scented with the sweet fragrance of incense.

Gompo, the eldest monk in the group, shifted his bony frame on the cushion he sat on and gave young Targye a hard look with eyes surrounded by a web of deep lines etched into his leathery skin by the wind and sun. The old monk had encountered many who were quick to brag about the psychic powers their faith provided them. Gompo doubted that Targye felt anything other than the gas in his intestines from the extra helping of barley he'd had for lunch. But the old monk remained silent; perhaps thinking the Buddha was nearby would inspire the others to do their best as they formulated plans for their suicidal mission.

The sound of metal drums and chanting from

the nearby religious service rattled through the cold air as Targye proceeded to speak. "Did you get a map of the ancient city where they have taken the Buddha?" he asked one of the monks.

The holy man produced an old scroll from his crimson robes. "We found this in the library," he answered. "It appears to be the plans for the original citadel. But whether the diagram was closely followed or if changes have been made to it since then—who knows?"

"Let me see it," Targye ordered, shifting several of the red candles burning in front of him to spread out the scroll. The wrinkled parchment was yellowed with age and had one edge blackened, as if it had almost been burned sometime in the past.

"The *bodhisattva* is in this area," he said in a low voice, his shaking finger tracing a pathway down a long hallway on the drawing. "They took him along this corridor—to here." His finger speared the tiny smudge at the end of the hall. "These tiny rooms—they are prison cells. The Buddha is in the last one."

Gompo could hold his tongue no longer. "I fear the hopefulness of youth may have caused you to imagine that somehow—"

"No!" Targye insisted, rudely interrupting the older monk. "The Buddha is here among us—I feel it. And he has shown me where he is."

"I admire your faith in the reincarnated one," Gompo said, deciding to take a more diplomatic course. "But we must double-check. Perhaps a demon has somehow—"

"Do not associate our *bodhisattva* with a demon," Targye warned.

"No, I do not say that." Gompo paused, and everyone waited for him to continue. "It is just that if you are somehow wrong, many of us will pay the price with our blood. You know the Chinese—"

"Targye is right," another monk interposed. "I feel his presence too. He is in that cell."

"I feel it also."

"And I."

Gompo knew better than to argue further. He closed his tired eyes and hoped he was wrong. But he felt no presence in the room other than the sweaty monks who sat around him.

"We are agreed, then?" Targye inquired, glaring at his elder.

Gompo nodded almost imperceptibly, glancing toward the parchment. His eyes narrowed as he studied it. *Was it possible?* It looked as if the map held more secrets of its own. He scanned the faces sitting beside him, his gaze stopping on Targye, whose eyes glowed red in the candlelight.

"We have no time to lose," the young monk told the others. "The Chinese will undoubtedly torture him, try to make him confess to crimes."

"Or use drugs," another suggested.

"Yes." Targye nodded. "But the Buddha will not give in. Eventually they will realize this and kill him. Then we will have to wait for the next reincarnation. We must rescue him or suffer a setback of years, perhaps a generation." He paused, studying the face of each one around him.

"I think I have found a way to accomplish our task," Gompo interjected before Targye could continue. Abruptly, the old monk was the center of attention and his younger competitor's face was clouded in anger. "If this diagram is correct, we may be able to attain the *bodhisattva*'s freedom with minimal risk."

Those around him leaned forward as Gompo's finger pointed to the ancient parchment. "This is what we could do," he began.

Death Song checked the Satellite Geographical Positioning System to find their exact location, then spoke over the MH-60K's intercom. "The SGPS says we're right on the money."

"Good," Oz responded, raising his NVG and rubbing his tired eyes. "O.T., alert our passenger; we're about to the drop point."

"Yes, sir."

The pilot surveyed the towering snowy peaks that rose around the desertlike area, which was inhabited only by herds of wild yaks—*drongs*—that grazed or chewed their cud and huddled together to ward off the night's chill and preying wolves. After the chopper had passed the base of Mount Everest, its peak invisible in a shroud of clouds, Oz dropped back into the Zangbo River valley.

A half hour later they passed a solitary horseman who searched the darkness for the strange whooping sound and felt his long hair mussed by the passing American aircraft, which he failed to locate in the night. The poor peasant, unable to see the passing helicopter, thought he'd been pursued by a demon.

The gales in the mountain passes were becoming treacherous, and the thin air slowed the chopper's response to the controls. Oz gripped the control column more tightly as they shot into the gorge straight ahead and climbed upward in the frosty atmosphere toward their destination. Though there had been no sign of Chinese radar, the pilot kept the chopper low for safety. The wind abruptly kicked the MH-60K, inducing it to shudder like a giant animal as the pilot fought for control of the machine, pushing it back onto its path.

Oz switched on the modified AN/ASC-15B triservice battlefield support system radio to contact the military communications satellite overhead. After receiving the helicopter's signal, the COMSAT interrogated the aircraft's computer for the proper codes, then transferred their carrier wave to Captain Louis Warner, the Night Stalkers' commander, who was halfway around the world at Fort Bragg, North Carolina.

The computer signaled the completion of the connection, and the pilot spoke through the complex link. "This is Buddha's Crown One. Over."

"Buddha's Crown One, I read you loud and clear," Warner answered.

"We're at checkpoint Alpha One and will complete the first phase of our mission in a few minutes. Are there any changes in plans? Over."

The pilot was greeted only by silence, and for a moment Oz sat tensely in the darkness, wondering if the COMSAT link had been lost or if the mission was about to be aborted.

"You have a go-ahead," Warner's voice finally advised him. "I say again, you have a go-ahead. Please verify. Over."

"I verify we have a go-ahead," Oz responded.

"Good luck, One," Warner said. "Over and out."

Oz toggled off his radio.

"Our LZ is dead ahead," Death Song announced, glancing up from the HSD screen after tapping a key on the chopper's computer console. "You're X-ringing it."

"O.T., Luger," Oz called over the intercom. "Have our dog ready and let's go in hot—arm your weapons. But do not fire unless we're fired on. We want to cause a minimum amount of trouble so our dog won't be detected."

Because the ferrying range of the MH-60K was only a maximum of three hundred kilometers, it carried external fuel tanks that allowed it to cover the long trip into Tibet without needing to refuel during the mission. But the external tank system had replaced the weapons pods, leaving only the Miniguns on either side of the chopper for defense. Oz felt vulnerable without the usual armament, but he directed his mind back to his duties. "Is Chung on the intercom?" he asked.

"Sure am, Captain," the agent's voice called. "What's all this 'dog' business?"

"What?" the pilot queried.

"You and your crew keep asking about 'the dog.'"

Oz laughed. "No offense. All passengers are called dogs—old flying tradition."

"I'm not sure I want to know how that tradition got started," Chung deadpanned. "I'll be ready to get out of the chopper as soon as you touch down."

"We'll take off as soon as you're out of the chopper's way," the pilot told him. "If things aren't right, radio at once and we'll come in and get you."

"Sounds good," Chung said. "If everything looks okay and I don't need a quick lift out, I'll click my radio off and on twice, pause, and then give you four more clicks. Once you receive that, the sooner you get out of the area, the better off we'll both be."

"Okay," Oz replied. "We'll keep low and as quiet as we can and get you out if you radio for help, or we'll beat a hasty retreat if we get two clicks followed by four from you."

"About one minute until touchdown," Death Song warned.

"Got that, Chung?" Oz asked.

"I'm as ready as I'm ever going to be," the agent replied, his voice slightly edgy.

"We'll be landing on a slope," Oz told him. "Go out on the low side of the chopper and remember to keep your head down and stay away from the tail rotor."

"I'll stay clear."

"Both our Miniguns are juiced back here," O.T. informed the pilot.

The darkness of the Himalayas loomed south of them, half hidden by drifting clouds of fog rendered light green by the pilot's night-vision goggles. Oz pulled the control column back and the MH-60K decelerated as they hurtled forward, skimming above the Zangbo River, which had carved out the valley below.

"I'm taking us in for a quick look," Oz warned the crew as the aircraft neared the earth. The dark river rolled along its twisting path, kicking white foam in the eddies of rock, which then dropped abruptly in tiny waterfalls. The wind surged, shoving the helicopter to the side before Oz straightened it back onto its course.

Locating a spot to set down, the pilot stomped on the right pedal and cramped the control column. The MH-60K responded sluggishly, lurching to the right and fighting the gust of air that dropped as convection currents from the distant mountains. He pulled on the control column slightly, finally bringing the chopper into a hover like a giant hummingbird in the thin mountain air.

There was no sign of human life in the area. "Anyone see anything?" the pilot quizzed his crew.

Death Song checked the forward-looking infrared scope as the others inspected the area. "The area looks clear on the FLIR."

"Clear back here," O.T. called.

"Ditto on that," Luger added.

"Hang on," Death Song said. "At two o'clock."

Oz directed the chopper toward the northwest, where his copilot had indicated, and scanned the area. "I see it," Oz said, dropping lower. Abruptly the shape ran down the rocky incline toward the river.

"A donkey?" O.T. asked from the back.

"Wild ass," Oz said. "Native fauna for the region."

"And I thought they only had those in Washington," O.T. muttered.

"Anyone see anything else?" the pilot asked.

"It looks clear," Death Song answered.

Oz circled the area once more, then swooped down toward the rocky slope. He bounced the chopper off the ground-effect turbulence from their blades as air pushed downward was reflected upward by the earth. Because of the possibility of the tail rotor striking the slanting mountainside during landing or takeoff, Oz swung his chopper around so that it was cross-slope. Then he held it in a hover for a moment and carefully positioned the MH-60K.

"See any obstacles?" he asked, glancing over his shoulder and checking behind the chopper.

"All clear," O.T. answered.

Oz lowered the collective pitch lever, dropping them slowly to the ground. He continued the descent until the left front wheel touched the rocks below, then shoved the control column to port, anchoring the wheel closest to him against the incline. He then quickly reduced the collective and continued to inch the column to the left until the remaining two wheels touched the earth.

The pilot shoved down on the collective pitch lever, leaving the rotors at their normal rotating speed so he could lift off immediately if the aircraft started to slide on the rocky slope. "All right, Chung, it's all yours. Exit from the down slope, starboard side."

Oz could hear the side door slide out of the way in the passenger compartment as O.T. pushed it aft on its runners.

"Thanks," Chung replied over the intercom. "I'll see you guys in a day or so."

"We'll be here," Oz promised. "Good luck."

The intercom popped as Chung removed his headphones and dropped them on his chair. Then he leapt out of the chopper and was lost in the darkness as he quickly made his way toward the crude roadway leading into Saga.

"All clear for takeoff," O.T. called as he slid the side door closed.

Oz lifted the chopper into the air, mindful of the wind currents that threatened to trip the chopper into a dynamic rollover. Once in the air, he searched the ground for some sign of the agent, but the CIA operative was nowhere to be seen.

The radio clicked twice; there was a pause, then four more clicks.

"Sounds like he didn't encounter any problems," Death Song remarked.

"Great," Oz replied. "Now let's get on our new heading for the trip home." He pushed at the control column and accelerated clear of the area to minimize the chances of Chung's being betrayed by the chopper's presence.

Death Song tapped the buttons alongside his virtual situation display, then poked another button on the edge of his second screen. His fingers stabbed at several keys on the chopper's computer console, and the device plotted their return course to the USS *America*, outlining it on the electronic map on the console.

*It will be a relief to get back to the ship,* Oz reflected, aligning the aircraft onto the new course. He was beat.

# 9

"NS-1, you are cleared to come on in to your parking space—it's reserved with your name painted on it. Over."

"Thank you, CV-66," Oz said, shaking his head at the would-be comic on the other end. "Our ETA is ten minutes. Over and out."

Oz felt like his back was about to break; his muscles were tied in knots. He promised himself a hot shower on the USS *America* after they finally got the chopper in and everything shut down.

*Hopefully we'll get some sleep before Chung needs to be picked up,* he thought. But that wouldn't necessarily be the case. It wasn't inconceivable that they'd have to go back after touching down and refueling. The pilot hoped that wouldn't happen—it sounded unbearable.

The USS *America* materialized as a dot ahead of them, at first appearing to be a bit of debris and then growing into a steel island gently rolling on the dark ocean. The deck blazed with lights, but the sun was only a hint in the east, where the sky was beginning to glow faintly in shades of pink and lavender.

In a few minutes the MH-60K descended onto the carrier's busy deck, where the activities of getting planes into the air, gear stowed, and aircraft moved up and down on lifts continued at nearly the same pace around the clock, day after day. Fifteen minutes later Oz and his crew emerged from the chopper, legs stiff from the flight.

"I don't envy Chung," O.T. remarked, pushing a wad of bubble gum into his mouth as he balanced his Colt carbine under one arm and his helmet under the other. "Sneaking around trying to find out who knows what with the Chinese trying to take you apart isn't my idea of a fun outing."

The others were too tired to respond. After checking that the helicopter was being refueled, the four airmen headed to their cabins for some much-needed sleep.

The sun appeared to melt the mists from the mountain peaks as Chung climbed onto the crude road leading to Saga. The devastation in the countryside was worse than the agent had been prepared for. He had known that during the Cultural Revolution of the 1960s the Chinese had destroyed thousands of monasteries and monuments. But as he trudged by the ruins of bricks, broken glass, and charred wood, the events of those years were brought into sharp focus, prompting him to realize that men, women, and children had been left homeless and had even died during the purges.

It also reminded him of the destruction he'd witnessed in Vietnam before fleeing with his family from the communists there.

An hour after journeying down the narrow gravel road, he overtook a group of *drokpas*. Slowing his pace, he stayed behind them, close enough to be mistaken—he hoped—for one of them. The twenty-odd *drokpa* nomads were dressed in ragged outfits similar to his own and appeared to be headed for Saga.

There were signs that the Dalai Lama's encouragement to return to the old ways was taking effect. Many of the men and women they passed on the roadway were chanting Buddhist prayers in low guttural tones, and several ancient Tibetan murals on huge boulders along the roadway had recently been repainted.

As he passed one such mural, Chung glanced up and studied the blue and white figures painted over a bright yellow background ringed in red. He recognized Shinje, the lord of death, dancing over the body of a fallen yak, which—if he recalled correctly—represented fleshly passions. The god wore a belt of human heads around his waist and held several objects whose symbolic meanings the agent didn't comprehend.

"Let me see your papers," a voice suddenly ordered.

Chung jerked his attention away from the mural and discovered a squad of Chinese troops in dark green uniforms blocking the roadway. The agent swore under his breath, cursing himself for not being more vigilant. He should have seen the squad before it stopped the group. Quickly looking downward to the mud and pebble surface of the roadway like the others in the group, he avoided meeting the eyes of the troops who menaced the Tibetans with the muzzles of their Type 79 submachine guns.

"Your papers—*now!*" the officer screamed at the leader of the *drokpas*.

The nomad fished under his threadbare jacket and produced a dog-eared leather booklet, which he handed over.

The Chinese jerked the document from the man's hand, opened it, and studied the papers inside. "Are you going to Saga?" he demanded.

"Yes," the *drokpa* answered in a high-pitched voice.

"What is your business there?"

"We are going to visit our relatives."

The officer stood silently for a few minutes, then hurled the document at the man's feet. "You may pass," he shouted.

The leader picked the booklet out of the dust and walked down the road, his face expressionless. The nomads filed past the officer, who studied each one as if searching for someone.

Chung held his breath as he came alongside the Chinese.

The soldier's eyes seemed to bore into the American.

"You!" he suddenly cried. "Give me your papers."

The agent's fingers snaked toward his hidden pistol, but he quickly thought better of it, realizing that the muzzles of nearly all the soldiers' weapons were trained on him and the Buddhist nomads. He stopped and turned toward the Chinese officer, his eyes lowered.

"Not you, fool," the soldier shrieked at Chung. "*You*, old man," he cried, pointing toward the wizened nomad just ahead of the agent. "Let me see your papers—if you have any."

Chung turned and made his way toward the rest of the group, covertly glancing at the old man, who handed soiled papers to the soldier. The cluster of Tibetans disregarded the old man in the same way yaks ignore one of their own after it has been culled from the herd by wolves. The nomads shuffled down the rocky pass and rounded the corner of the road, leaving the soldiers and the old man behind.

The agent shakily stepped off the gravel roadway and collapsed onto a rounded boulder nestled in a mound of scrub brush. His stomach churned, and for a moment he felt as if he'd be sick as he sat there. After several minutes he finally regained his composure and stood up, deciding he'd better catch up with the group, which was now far ahead of him.

"That was a close call," a voice said in Tibetan as the agent stepped back onto the roadway.

Chung glanced around and saw the old man the Chinese soldiers had stopped trudging up the roadway, a gnarled staff helping to support his weight as he shuffled toward the agent. "My papers were in order—more than you can say, I'd wager."

"You may be right, my old friend," Chung said cautiously.

The nomad smiled, his cracked lips parting to reveal two lone teeth that looked like kernels left behind on a well-chewed cob of corn. "I am Gompo," the old man said. "Stick close to me. I'll help you get to Saga. That is where you're headed?"

"Yes." Chung nodded. "Here, let me carry your pack."

The Buddhist monk strolled beside the American agent as they entered the outskirts of Saga, wondering who the stranger beside him was and where he was from. That it was more than chance the two men had met, Gompo was sure. The stranger's accent was good, but it suggested a hint of some other language—English, the old man guessed. It occurred to the monk that the young man might be a Chinese agent, but certainly the stranger's fear at the checkpoint had seemed genuine enough, so Gompo dismissed the idea.

*What did that leave?* he wondered.

"Where do all these soldiers come from?" Chung asked, dodging a yak-pulled cart full of untanned leather as it rattled past.

"Up there." Gompo pointed with a gnarled finger toward the mountain peak that towered over the town. "They've taken over the old monastery up there and turned it into their fortress. Big mechanical birds come and go from there day and night. The villagers say they have desecrated the holy place and transformed it into a prison. I believe that is where our Dalai Lama is being held."

Chung surveyed his companion from the corner of his eye.

*I have said too much,* Gompo thought to himself, noting the quizzical look on the stranger's face.

"Do the soldiers ever come into the village?" Chung asked, his voice barely audible over the haggling of two merchants who held a string of silver beads.

"The soldiers come down from their roost like buzzards—to eat and drink," Gompo replied. "The villagers don't like it, but they don't dare slight the troops for fear of retaliation. The Chinese have weapons on that mountain that could destroy the village in a few moments. Some say they have poison gases like those used in Lhasa."

The two men were silent for a few moments, and then the stranger's eyes fastened on the lone soldier walking down the street toward them. "Gompo, I must leave you now," the agent said. "Take this for good luck." Chung fished in his pocket, produced a gold coin, and pressed it into the old man's hand.

"I have no need of this," Gompo protested, wondering how the stranger could have come to possess the small fortune and then be so quick to part with it.

"Keep it," Chung said, stepping back from the old man before the gold piece could be returned. "It is not too much for a new friend who saved my life."

"I feel I will see you again." Gompo smiled. "If not in this life, then in our reincarnations." The old man grasped the coin tightly.

"Perhaps you will," Chung acknowledged.

"The Buddha protect you," Gompo intoned, his hands tracing a holy sign in the air as he spoke.

Chung again looked puzzled, as if wondering why a nomad would bless him as only a Buddhist monk would. But then the agent turned quickly away, seeming to forget the incongruity as he pursued the lone Chinese soldier who had turned a dusty corner onto a narrow street. The man suddenly vanished behind a mud brick hut decorated with brightly painted Buddhist prayer wheels nestled in its wall.

*Unless I'm greatly mistaken,* Gompo thought, watching the agent slink down the street, carefully avoiding the soldier's gaze, *that man is stalking the Chinese trooper.*

What was going on? Perhaps the *bodhisattva* had guided the monk to someone who was an ally. The holy man shook his head in disgust. *I'm beginning to think like Targye,* Gompo chastised himself. More than likely the stranger was a drug peddler or a pimp, looking for a sale.

But Gompo followed in the two men's footsteps anyway. There was something about the stranger, and maybe he *had* been sent by the Buddha.

# 10

In the bunk of the windowless gray cabin reserved for him, Oz instantly fell asleep after returning to the USS *America,* too tired even to remove his boots. He dozed fitfully for three hours before jerking awake, thinking he had fallen asleep at the controls of the helicopter. For a moment he lay there in the bunk, unable to recall where he was; then he relaxed, wide awake with the adrenaline generated by fear coursing through his veins.

He'd had the dream before and knew he couldn't go back to sleep. *Might as well get up,* he thought resignedly. Rolling over, he blinked in the cabin's dim light and checked his watch. *Almost noon.* His stomach felt empty, sore, and hungry.

He threw his legs over the edge of the bunk, realizing he still had his boots on as they landed on the steel deck. He glanced around and noticed Death Song and Luger still asleep in their bunks. O.T., who seemed to require very little sleep, was nowhere to be seen.

*Probably bugging some sailor to play a game of chess.* Oz smiled to himself.

After a shower and a change of clothing, the pilot made his way through the bowels of the giant aircraft carrier toward the officers' mess. As it was at all times of the day and night, the ship, with its crew of two thousand and a two-thousand-plus air wing, was a beehive of activity.

After winding down one last steel corridor, Oz reached the mess, where he helped himself to a salad and a slice of apple pie, a serving of mashed potatoes, and what the sailors in front of him referred to as "mystery meat."

After pouring himself a cup of coffee, he spied an empty table and headed for it, hoping to get through the meal without having to answer questions from some curious officer wondering what type of mission he was on. While it was simple enough to say the information was secret, he'd found that many questioners took offense at that answer for reasons he'd never fully understood. It was easier simply to avoid such confrontations.

Settling onto the bench, he sipped the hot coffee, hoping it would drive away some of his fatigue.

"How about some company?" a familiar voice asked in a Brooklyn accent.

Oz glanced up at a pock-scarred face. "Commander Warner!" he exclaimed, relieved that he wasn't facing a potential naval interrogator. "What in the world are you doing here?"

The officer set his tray on the table across from the pilot and eased himself onto the bench. After double-checking that no one at the nearby tables could overhear, Warner answered. "Looks like the CIA's getting ready to have you go into Tibet. Probably to pull someone out besides the agent you ferried in last night. I don't have the details yet, but I'm guessing we're supporting the move for Tibetan independence. I'm supposed to get my orders in about an hour, and I'll brief you then—along with the other three Night Stalker crews and Delta Force officers who just came in fifteen minutes ago."

"Sounds like things are going to get interesting," the pilot mused.

"You can bet on that." Warner nodded, tearing a roll apart and slathering a hunk of butter on it.

Chung landed an expert punch on the back of the Chinese soldier, rendering the trooper instantly unconscious. *Thank goodness this guy's small,* the agent thought, throwing the limp body over his shoulder and staggering toward the shop he'd just passed.

The toothless shop owner gazed at the agent and his burden as they tottered through the front door.

"The flag on the front of your shop shows you have a room?" the agent asked in flawless Tibetan.

The shop owner didn't want to commit himself. "Perhaps there's a room. But I want no trouble."

"No trouble. My friend here has had a bit too much to drink. If I can get him a room so his commanding officer won't find out about his little problem with alcohol—you know how these Chinese soldiers are."

"I don't think that it would be a good idea."

The shop owner paused as his green eyes fastened onto Chung's hand, which was fishing inside his coat. The hand reappeared with a cloth bag that the agent tossed onto the low countertop where the proprietor sat cross-legged. The bag jingled unmistakably.

"That's yours if I can have the room for just a few hours," Chung said. "Then we will be gone and in your debt. No one need ever know that we were here."

The shopkeeper opened the bag and beamed at the sight of the small fortune in gold coins twinkling inside. The bag disappeared under the rags he wore. "Quickly. Get him out of sight," he directed, motioning toward the curtain at the back of the room. "Up the steps. The only room up there. Be out in three hours."

"We will."

The agent half carried, half dragged the soldier up the chipped stone stairway into a tiny room little bigger than a closet. Sunlight streamed through the cracks in the shutter on the window, lighting the dust motes that floated in the chilly air. Chung scooted the soldier toward the rag-covered cot that was the only furniture in the cubicle and awkwardly lowered the inert form onto it, lifting the trooper's booted feet so the unconscious man was stretched out as if asleep.

Chung then rapidly removed the hypodermic kit from his clothing and, estimating the weight of the slight soldier to adjust the dose, set the hypodermic syringe to the proper amount and inserted the needle through the rubber stopper of the upturned bottle of sodium pentothal. He pumped the air into the bottle, and it bubbled into the container, increasing the air pressure inside the bottle and making it easy to draw the oily liquid into the syringe.

The agent replaced the bottle in its holder, knelt

beside the soldier, and pulled up his sleeve. The trooper groaned as the agent plunged the needle into his arm.

*Perfect timing,* Chung told himself as the man's eyes fluttered open. A few more minutes and he would have had a fight on his hands.

After waiting a few minutes, the agent spoke in Chinese to the soldier. "Who are you and what is your rank?"

"I am Hsing Yung," the man said in a monotone.

"Rank?"

The soldier closed his eyes, then stared at the ceiling. "Private in the People's Army of China."

The agent smiled. The drug was working, and the subject was speaking freely, not even realizing he was being interrogated. Unlike western agents, who often resisted sodium pentothal, soldiers in oppressive societies were used to taking orders. They made good subjects for drug-assisted interrogations.

"Private Hsing Yung, think carefully. Where is the Dalai Lama?"

"Sometimes he is in the cell in our citadel. Sometimes he vanishes."

"What citadel?"

"Ours—above the village of Saga."

"What do you mean 'sometimes he vanishes'?"

The soldier's face twisted as if he were in pain.

"Relax," Chung ordered. "Just tell me what you've heard."

"The guard who watched him last night found his cell empty. One minute the holy man was there, the next, gone. It is impossible to dissolve and flow through iron and stone, and yet the holy man seems to do it."

"But he's there now, in the fortress?"

"He always comes back. He can't seem to escape for long. Not yet. But the soldiers are fearful that he has other powers that will bring us down."

*This sounds crazy,* the agent thought, rising to his feet. Probably the drugs were affecting the soldier's ability to reason, though Chung had never heard of such a reaction to sodium pentothal. At any rate, he had what he'd come for.

He rolled up his pants leg and ripped the radio loose from the tape that held it to his calf. Then he pulled out the antenna, set the selector to COMSAT, and lifted the cover over the power switch. He toggled the radio on; a red LED glowed to life, and a soft beep told him it was automatically attempting to uplink with the communications satellite that hung far above Chung in geosynchronous orbit.

But the red light remained on rather than turning green, and the unit beeped a warning that it had failed to link up with the satellite.

*What's wrong?* the agent wondered impatiently. He switched the unit off and on and waited a few minutes for it to attempt another link, but it still refused to bond to the satellite above.

*What the hell's wrong with this thing?* Chung pondered, shaking the radio. The LED showed that the batteries were charged, and it seemed to be working, but it wasn't connecting.

A commotion of cries and angry protests in the street distracted his attention. Chung crossed to the shuttered window and peered through the cracks onto the dusty street below.

A squad of Chinese soldiers carrying rifles with spiked bayonets charged down the street, prompting the civilians in the narrow avenue to scatter in all directions. The twelve troopers stormed toward the shop where the agent was hidden.


Major Ling paced the corridor of the frosty citadel, snorting a cloud of fog with each breath like some kind of dragon. He pulled his cloak around his shivering frame, amazed that the granite building could resist the day's attempt to warm it with sunlight. The smokey braziers his soldiers had set up had proved to be equally ineffective in warming the fortress.

*What is going on in the village?* he fretted, pacing to the window that overlooked the squalor below. Saga spread out beneath him like a toy city some mad child had fashioned out of rock and mud, streets winding around the hillside on which the town was built, often ending unexpectedly or jogging off to the side.

He'd know soon enough, once Woo and his troops had located Hsing Yung. First his messenger had vanished. Then a shop owner had come to the entrance of the fortress, informing the guards that a stranger had taken an unconscious Chinese soldier upstairs to a room in his shop to do who knew what to the man.

*If they break in and find them in a lovers' embrace, it would be a relief,* Ling thought, smiling grimly to himself. He'd rather shoot one of his men for homosexual acts than discover that the Buddhists were aware that the Dalai Lama was in the village and were formulating a rescue plan by pumping one of his men.

*That would be nonsense,* the officer reminded himself. It was impossible that the religious zealots knew the Buddha was in Saga—unless he really could evaporate from his cell and travel through space.

The major laughed.

His men would have him believe that. But his soldiers were ignorant peasants to the last man; even Woo acted as if he'd started having second thoughts about whether the prisoner was a mere mortal.

But they'd change their minds once he'd finished with the Dalai Lama; then the monk would either be mad or be working for the Chinese. *It's amazing what drugs and the judicious application of pain can bring about,* he reflected. And he was just the expert for such a task.

Then his soldiers would see that science and the state were more powerful than the opiate of the people. Yes, the Buddha would be broken, and they'd all see how powerful the people's government could be.

But if the Buddhists didn't know where the Dalai Lama was, then who was the stranger with Hsing Yung? And why hadn't his informant contacted him? Ling smashed his fist into the open palm of his other hand, impatient to get to the bottom of both mysteries.

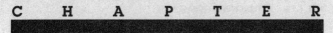
Each of the monks knew that the secret meeting in the ruins below Major Ling's fortress was dangerous, but it was the safest place in Saga, possibly the last place the Chinese soldiers would suspect, simply because it was so close to their stronghold. The nineteen monks sat in a circle, one of their members missing after failing to make it past the Chinese checkpoint just outside Tradom.

Sunlight filtered through the holes in the nearly collapsed roof above them, creating beams that looked solid, delineated by the smoke from the incense sticks burning around the clerics; the Buddhists were risking discovery with the fragrant incense sticks and their soft chanting, but they felt them essential and hoped the wind blowing away from the fortress would protect them from detection.

After the ceremony they finalized their dangerous plans. "So my best guess is that the stranger I met is an American or Soviet agent," Gompo finished after telling the others about the man he had met on the road to Saga.

"Perhaps we should try to contact this stranger

and join forces with him," Amdma suggested, his innocent eyes glowing bright blue in a beam of sunlight.

"I am not sure that would be wise," Gompo dissented. "We don't know what the Americans or Soviets may be planning or how soon they will act."

"If they even bother to act," Targye added. "They are interested in thwarting the Chinese. They may help us if we fit into their plans, but we can't depend on it. Besides, now that we know the secret of the parchment, we can—"

"I just thought. . ." Amdma's voice trailed off.

"We need every idea," Gompo reassured the young man, smiling to expose his two teeth. "But it's important to remember that not everyone walking the same direction is aspiring toward the same place or searching for the same thing."

"We know the *bodhisattva* is up there," Targye said, guiding them back to their rescue plans. "The villagers have overheard the soldiers talking about him. And the Chinese are upset by the miracles the Dalai Lama works, even locked in a cell of stone and iron. I say now is the time to strike, before they decide to harm him."

The others were quiet, studying Gompo to see what his response would be. Finally the old man spoke. "I agree." He nodded, throwing in his lot with Targye instead of arguing with him as he normally did. "With the secret we discovered on the map, we stand a good chance of success. And we don't have time to waste; those who were to meet us will be exposed on the plain. If the Dalai Lama doesn't reach them before the Chinese learn of the meeting, there will probably be a bloodbath."

"Then it is time to rescue the Buddha," Targye said.

One by one the others in the circle murmured agreement or nodded.

"Then it is settled," Targye announced. "Tonight we will free the *bodhisattva* from his worldly captors."

*Or die in the attempt,* Gompo reflected to himself. The secret they had discovered gave them an edge, but the monk was not certain such an advantage carried much weight in a world ruled by so many cruel gods and demons whose servants were Chinese with modern weapons.

Watching the soldiers on the street below, Chung drew his P7 pistol as he peeked through the crack in the shutter. Abruptly he became aware of a beeping sound, then a tinny voice: "This is Home Base. Go ahead, Shortstop. Over."

The CIA agent gaped at the transmitter. The green LED was blinking, signaling that it had linked to the communications satellite.

Why was it working now? he fretted. *The roof!* he realized. The tile roof on the building must have been stopping his transmissions. Moving to the shutters had gotten him clear of the obstruction, and as he watched the approaching Chinese soldiers, the transmitter had continued trying to connect to the satellite. Finally it had succeeded.

"This is Home Base. Can you read us, Shortstop?" the message repeated.

The startled agent thumbed the send button and spoke into the transmitter. "This is Shortstop, Home Base. I read you loud and clear. Over."

"Have you reached the wrong number? Over."

"T-4-6, S-2-5," Chung whispered into the transponder, giving the proper code to the CIA radio operator receiving the signal, reassuring him that it was actually Chung on the other end. The agent was aware of a commotion in the shop below as the soldiers pushed over tables in their haste to reach the stairs leading to the room where he was hiding. "The Big Egg is here. Repeat, the Big Egg is here. Did you get that, Home Base?"

"Roger, Shortstop. The Big Egg is there. We'll have your pickup in ASAP at location A if that's still a go. Over."

Boots clattered on the steps. "Negative, negative," Chung protested. "Do not send in an airlift— I've been discovered."

"Shortstop is—"

"Do not send anyone in for me!" the agent insisted.

The door inched ajar, and the agent whirled and fired his pistol, its discharge creating a cloud of dust and smoke in the room. His ringing ears discerned a muffled cry of pain behind the wooden door which now sported a 9mm bullet hole in its bulk.

Chung ducked at the flurry of gunfire from the stairwell, the barrage of bullets ripping holes in the door, showering him with a hail of splinters.

The agent fired three more quick shots through the aperture, then turned and pushed open the shutters of the window. Blinking in the sunlight that streamed into the room, he ducked as a second barrage of heavy bullets from the Chinese rifles slashed past him, chipping at the mud walls of the room.

He swallowed hard, then leapt through the shuttered window toward the street below. As he plum-

meted to earth, he fought to regain his balance
before striking the rocky surface but failed.
Groaning in pain, he felt the bones in his ankle shat-
ter with an audible snap as he hit.

The surprised Chinese soldier guarding the
entrance jabbed at the agent with his bayonet, but
Chung rolled out of reach, came to a stop, and fired
his pistol at the trooper. The single shot connected
with the man's chest, downing him almost instantly as
the fragmenting projectile cut into his heart and lungs.

Chung stumbled to his feet and then fell, stifling
a cry of pain. He pulled himself up again by gripping
the door frame, then hopped on his good foot down
the street, feeling slightly foolish yet knowing there
was no other way to place any distance between
himself and the soldiers who would soon be pursuing him.

As if to confirm his worst fears, a salvo of bullets
clipped the wall alongside his head as he bounded
like a kangaroo on his good leg. He slipped on a
loose rock and nearly fell but quickly regained his
balance and bounced around the corner of the building. As he started down a narrow street, the clatter
of boots echoed on the rocks behind him.

The street ahead was filled with villagers who
seemed frozen in place, wondering what the sudden
commotion was about. The agent sprang toward
them on his good foot, a silly grin on his face as he
realized what a ridiculous picture he must present.

The throng remained motionless until a young
woman noticed the pistol he was carrying,
screamed, snatched up her toddler in fear, and
began running. Her response created a chain reaction: The curious villagers suddenly regained their

motility and stampeded away from the approaching stranger with cries of terror.

By the time the American reached the center of the street, only a single bewildered beggar remained, a bowl of small coins in his hand as he stared up at the approaching agent. Not knowing what else to do, the destitute man held out his bowl expectantly.

"Sorry," the American apologized, pausing to snatch the crutch of the one-legged beggar. Placing its padded end under his armpit, the agent grimaced in pain as he rested his weight on the crutch and half slid, half hopped down the street with renewed speed.

Another volley of bullets cracked past Chung as he ducked into a shop crammed with new and used pots of all sizes and shapes. Resting his hand against the wall, he looked back toward the band of soldiers charging after him.

"Please get out!" the young female shopkeeper cried, unable to take her eyes off the gun held tightly in his fist. "Please leave! Please—" She was abruptly cut off as a bullet slammed into her forehead, nearly decapitating her and creating a cloud of flesh and bone that sprayed into the air and spattered the wares around her.

Chung swore as she fell, blinking in the cloud of blood that flecked his face. He ducked as four more shots thundered through the store. Dropping to his hands and knees, he crawled down the aisle, dragging his bad foot and the crutch behind him, his gun still held tightly in his fist. He paused and turned around, holding up his P7 pistol as he rose to his knees.

A green-capped face peered through the entrance into the store.

The agent fired and was pleased to see his bullet connect. Then he dived back down and crawled toward the rear of the store, searching for an avenue of escape.

A glimmer of sunlight shone from behind the tattered edges of a curtain that hung along the back wall. *A back entrance,* he thought, skinning his knuckles against the rough wood as he hastened on.

Suddenly the crutch caught on a shelf of pots, knocking it over; a brass caldron clanged noisily to the floor, rolling behind him, and several pottery vessels fragmented into hundreds of shards as he pushed past the curtain.

"Halt!" a voice ordered from behind him, a bullet crashing through the fabric above his head.

Ignoring the order, Chung hastily lowered the curtain behind him and rose to his feet, placing his weight on the crutch as he gawked at his surroundings and searched for the source of the sunlight.

He found himself inside a crude living space with blankets and pillows constituting its only furniture. The sunlight came from a skylight above him— too far to reach, especially with his bad ankle.

Hearing the soldiers fast approaching, he fired three quick shots through the curtain and was satisfied to hear a body falling onto a shelf of pots, creating a tumult of noise.

*There must be another way out,* he gritted to himself.

Glancing around, he spotted a runty child attempting to hide behind the largest of the cushions on the floor. *The shopkeeper's child,* the agent realized despondently, but quickly pushed the thought out of his mind. He could do nothing to alter the fact that she was dead. "Is there a way out of here?" Chung asked in Tibetan.

The frightened youngster pointed toward a large quilt hanging on the back wall.

The agent stumbled toward it, the noise of the soldiers' boots crackling on the broken pottery. He yanked the quilt away and found a window frame without a single pane in it. Without a second thought, he threw himself through the opening.

At the same instant gunfire thundered behind him. Dropping to the ground, he rolled in the dirt beyond the window, accidentally releasing his gun as he fell. He writhed in agony momentarily as a searing pain ran down his left arm. Knowing he was lost without a means to defend himself, he regained his composure, ignored his pain, and clawed his way over the dirt and gravel until his fingers grasped the weapon.

A plume of dirt exploded in front of him, kicking dirt into his eyes. As he blinked the grit away, he rolled over and faced the window, where a Chinese soldier leveled his rifle at him for a second shot.

Chung raised his P7 pistol, his finger tightening on the trigger, and fired the gun. The soldier fell backward, a bloody hole in his tunic.

The American took a deep breath, keeping his gun pointed toward the window. As he expected, a wary face peered out of the opening, and the agent fired again, plugging the soldier in the forehead.

*That should make them a bit more cautious,* Chung thought, struggling upright and doing his best to ignore the blood that poured from the gunshot wound in his left arm. The pain in both his ankle and his arm was gone, but he knew that wasn't a good sign; he must be going into shock. He'd have to get medical treatment soon, plus he'd undoubtedly faint if he didn't find a place to sit down.

*But first you have to escape,* he reminded himself, shaking his head in an effort to clear it. He continued down the alleyway, crutch thumping against the flat stones that formed a rough pavement under him. *If I can just make this corner, I might be able to lose them,* he reasoned.

"Put the gun down!" a voice instructed from behind.

*Keep going,* the agent ordered himself, straining toward his goal.

Four expressionless soldiers stepped out in front of him and blocked the end of the alley, bayonets pointed toward his chest.

The agent stopped and hobbled backward, balanced precariously on his crutch. He turned around and discovered three other soldiers with the muzzles of their Type 81 rifles leveled at him. For a moment he wondered: If the soldiers behind him fired, how many of the troops in front of him would be hit? Then he decided it didn't make any difference.

*The loss of blood is making you punchy,* he warned himself. *This isn't a game.*

Lieutenant Woo, the Chinese officer, stepped out in front of his riflemen, pistol held casually in his fist. "Put your firearm down and come quietly," he directed. "There's no need for anyone else to get hurt."

The American stood balanced on his good leg and the crutch, blood running into the dust. He felt faint and realized he must act quickly or the Chinese would have him; already he could see out of the corner of his eye that the four with bayonets were quietly approaching from behind.

*There is one way out,* he reminded himself, his light-headedness making his idea seem somehow funny.

"Everything will be all right," Woo reassured him, taking a step toward the agent, who appeared to be about to release his pistol. "Put down the gun."

"Stay back," Chung warned, waving his pistol and grinning at the soldier. Speaking in English, he added, "Go to hell."

Woo froze in place, studying the agent's face as if trying to discern what kind of trick the spy might be trying to pull and wondering what he had just said to them. "Don't try any tricks—" the Chinese officer warned.

The American agent raised his pistol, fingers tightening to release the grip safety.

"—or we will be forced to kill you," the soldier added.

The agent flashed him another grin, placed the muzzle against the base of his neck, and jerked the trigger before Woo or his men could stop him.

# 12

"So God is alive and well but imprisoned in Saga," Lieutenant Sudden Tomlin quipped after Commander Warner had summed up the various assignments at the beginning of the briefing aboard the USS *America*.

"That's about it," Warner agreed after the snickers had subsided. "But I want you to know that this information probably cost at least one man—our CIA agent in Tibet—his life. It may sound funny to you, but we need to be dead serious about Operation Buddha's Crown."

"Yes, sir," Sudden replied, abruptly sober.

"Now, our three MH-60Ks will carry your Delta Force squad over roughly the same route Captain Carson took to drop off agent Chung, since we have no reason to believe it was compromised. It would be better to have a new route, but as you can see, there aren't many paths available through the mountains. If we go any higher, we'll run into severe operational problems with our choppers.

"While the two Apache gunships accompanying you will carry plenty of firepower, we're going to have the MH-60Ks fully armed as well," Warner continued. "That means they'll have to convey fuel bladders in with them. Satellite surveillance has located one of the ruins of a lamasery the Chinese destroyed twenty years ago—here near Phuntsogling." He pointed on the computer-generated map on the large screen behind him. "You can refuel before going into Saga and, if time and conditions permit, refuel on the way out."

"We'll have just enough to make it back if we can't refuel," Oz said.

"*If* you don't run into any trouble," Warner qualified. "But if you're forced to take an alternate route or engage the enemy for any length of time, you'll never make it back into neutral territory. So if possible, I'd like to see you refuel."

The commander turned back to the screen and spent the next few minutes reviewing the details of the plans for the actual assault on the fortress as well as handing out photos of the Dalai Lama so the troops entering the citadel would recognize him. After making a few last-minute changes suggested by Sudden and Oz, the commander finished the briefing. "All right, then, if there are no further questions, I think that about covers it." He paused a moment, tapping a cigarette out of the ever-present pack in his pocket. "Get your men ready and briefed. I have you cleared to leave the USS *America* at nineteen hundred hours. Good luck."

"As cold as this place is, it makes an ideal mortuary," Major Ling remarked to Lieutenant Woo and the medic as the three stood together in the nearly empty room.

He was happy to see that neither soldier smiled; they must be unsure whether he was joking, and it pleased him to keep his men a little off balance. *Complacency breeds incompetence,* he thought as he inspected the naked corpse on the table one more time, willing some clue to be there.

But there was no clue to be found. No tattoos. One scar on the man's leg and another two-inch one on his left arm, nearly obscured by the rifle bullet wound the man had suffered just before his death; it was impossible to tell what had caused the two scars, which must have occurred years before.

His self-inflicted gunshot wound to the head had destroyed much of his face but made his dental work easy to inspect. The dental work was good, certainly not the type of work a peasant in either China or Tibet could expect to receive. A porcelain cap on a rear molar suggested some sophisticated technology and expense, and four teeth showed small fillings. But the dental work only ruled out a few regions of the world, and even in those areas the rich might travel abroad to obtain skilled dental treatment.

The major turned his back on the corpse and paced to the table containing the man's clothing and other possessions. The wearing apparel appeared identical to what half the citizens in the village wore, but perhaps it was a bit cleaner. The pistol the dead man had used so effectively was void of all markings, including those of a manufacturer, and a serial number; even the cartridges lacked head case marks.

The dead man carried no papers, and the transmitter found in his room also lacked distinguishing features except for "Made in Japan" printed on its IC circuits; the device itself was nonfunctional, since one of his clumsy men had managed to smash it under his boot during the pursuit of the agent. So there was no chance of turning it on to see if anyone would try to communicate with them. His electronics repairman was unfamiliar with the circuits in the device, making it beyond repair.

But the lack of ID and the advanced equipment left clues in and of themselves. Only a few countries could manage such feats; possibly the British or French but, more likely, the Soviets or Americans. "Are you sure he spoke perfect Chinese?" the major asked Woo.

"Yes, sir. No trace of an accent," the lieutenant answered. "Except for the last—"

"What do you mean?" Ling demanded.

"He mumbled something just before he shot himself. But none of us could understand it. Perhaps it was simply some mad ravings."

"Or perhaps he spoke in his own language before he killed himself," the major suggested. "Think hard; what did he say?"

"'Gotta Hall,'" Woo said after a moment. "Or something like that. 'Gootoo hell,' maybe." His face contorted. "More like 'gootoo hell,' I think."

"Go to hell," Ling said after a moment's thought.

"Yes, that's it." Woo nodded, surprised his commander would be familiar with the cryptic sounds. "What does it mean?"

"It means the Americans may know—or at least suspect—that we are keeping the Dalai Lama here," Ling replied softly, stroking his chin as he paced alongside the dead agent's body.

"Should we move our prisoner to a safer location?"

"Not yet. We don't know for sure the American got a message back to his people," Ling said. *And I also don't want to look like I'm running from danger,* he added to himself. Which was exactly what it would look like if he did anything now, before there was any concrete proof that the Americans were actually going to try anything. "In the interest of being careful we will double the guards on the walls and place patrols at either end of the village to double-check everyone coming or going. Hopefully we'll hear from our informant soon so we will know what the Buddhist monks may be up to."

Ling turned away from the officer, signaling that their meeting was over. The major studied the corpse as Woo's boots echoed down the hallway behind him. "Get rid of the body," he told the medic.

"Yes, sir," the subordinate answered, forgetting to salute as the officer turned to go; the soldier bowed instead.

*Peasants,* Ling snarled to himself as he left the chamber. He headed for the radio room, considering what he should do next. *There aren't too many mountain passes their transport helicopters can use to get into this area,* he reasoned. If the United States was trying to get more agents in, perhaps the Chinese Air Force could ambush them as they came into Tibet. Certainly the Chinese military leaders were eager for revenge after the Americans' sneak attack on their chemical weapons plant.

*Perhaps that can be used to my advantage.* He smiled to himself.

\*   \*   \*

The Night Stalkers flight teams and the Delta Force troops filed toward their helicopters, which were positioned on the port extension of the flight deck. The four-acre airstrip of the USS *America* rolled under Oz's feet, buoyed by the Indian Ocean, which seemed to be swallowing the glowing orb of the sun to the west.

An F-14A Tomcat thundered in, skipping across the flight deck and finally hooking the arresting wire that stretched behind the aircraft, bringing it to an abrupt halt before it could travel off the end of the landing strip. Flight crews rapidly vacated their protective positions along the edge of the deck to guide the plane to its parking position so another jet could land.

Two pairs of the Night Stalkers pilots headed for the McDonnell Douglas AH-64 Apache gunships; the gunner climbed into the front compartment while the pilot sat behind him, their tandem placement making the aircraft narrow and less vulnerable to enemy fire. First introduced into the army in 1984, the Apache had proved itself as a weapons system during the 1991 Gulf War.

Each Apache gunship had two stub wings extending from its sides; these provided extra lift and also held eight laser-guided Hellfire missiles with a range of almost four miles as well as auxiliary fuel tanks for the extended mission. Under the chin of the aircraft sat a remote-controlled 30mm chain gun slaved to a helmet control system the gunner wore. The weapons, coupled with the forward-looking infrared and Longbow radar systems of the aircraft, could pick out and hit targets in daylight or total darkness during all types of weather. Though the helicopters required careful maintenance work to keep them going, the Army felt the capable aircraft were worth the extra bother.

Like the MH-60Ks that would carry the Delta Force squads, the Apaches had boron-carbide-Kevlar composite armor and were capable of sustaining a variety of hits up to and including .50-caliber rounds and 14.5mm armor-piercing rounds.

Oz inspected his MH-60K before climbing in. The weapons pods mounted on the modified external tank suite struts carried what had become the Night Stalkers' usual armament: On the right side of the rack was a double 7.62mm machine gun pod with a twelve-tube 2.75-inch rocket launcher pod next to it; on the left was a 532 countermeasure dispenser to defeat heat-seeking as well as radar-guided missiles, with the last position filled with four Hellfire missiles similar to those the Apaches carried. The door gunners on each side of the helicopters manned 7.62mm Miniguns for additional suppressing fire.

The Delta Force troops climbing into the passenger compartments of the MH-60Ks carried a variety of weapons, from Colt M16A3 rifles to M203 grenade launchers and Minimi machine guns. In addition to their primary weapons, the soldiers carried stun and fragmentation grenades plus a variety of knives and pistols, most chosen to suit the tastes of the individual soldier. Several carried LAW rocket launchers, and three of the soldiers sported silenced Ruger Mark II pistols.

Oz donned his helmet and climbed into the chopper. After stowing his PK-15 submachine gun in its carrier behind his seat, he snapped the wire running from his helmet into the intercom system. "All right, let's get this bird wound up," he told his copilot.

"Yes, sir," Death Song answered. "We're ready to rock and roll."

It had been like a miracle, Norbu reflected, watching the stars twinkle over the barren plain where he sat. Men and even women from all over Tibet were assembling at the secret meeting place as word spread that the Dalai Lama would appear there soon to lead his people in the final conflict that would expel the Chinese from their land.

It sounded too good to be true, but Norbu would never know—he'd be too late to take part in the uprising.

What they had hoped would be a shortcut had turned out to be a pass choked with snow. Now they were at least a day's march from the meeting place. Since the Dalai Lama was to arrive there early the next day, Norbu and the others who huddled together for warmth in the darkness would miss him.

*We might still catch up, but again, we might not,* he reflected, fingering the old flintlock rifle his father had given him for the journey. Around him men were armed with similar crude weapons and a sprinkling of more modern rifles and pistols, many taken from Chinese soldiers whose weighted bodies now lay hidden in lakes or rivers after their throats had been cut.

In the darkness he could hear the clanking of metal firearms. "Victory to the gods," the approaching group yelled. The traditional Tibetan call offered to the supernatural beings that lived in and protected the mountains had taken on a new meaning: Now it was the code among the rebel bands that predicted the time when the king of gods, the Dalai Lama, would expel the Chinese from Tibet and take his place on the throne of the cradle of the world.

*So someone else made the same mistake we did,* the rebel thought glumly as the new group of rebels came up the slope and was welcomed by Norbu's party in the dark camp. *If this many of us weren't able to get to the meeting place, how many did?* he wondered despondently. The steady trickle of insurgents collecting on the plateau must by now be a large pool, ready to flood over the Chinese. *Perhaps, just perhaps, this will be the time we regain our freedom.*

Perhaps. But he wouldn't have any part in it because he would be a day late in getting there. He kicked at a rock. It had seemed too good to be true that he would be part of the historic work; he didn't dare hope for better luck for fear that a demon would hear his thoughts and conspire to make things even worse for him.

# 13

"Yes, it's here, just as the map shows," Gompo exulted, lifting one of the heavy rocks and quietly handing it to Amdma, who stood next to him.

The young priest grunted, passing the stone to the monk next to him, who transferred it down the line of monks. Gompo felt for another rock in the darkness, his fingers covered with blisters and cuts. Instead of a cold stone, however, his fingernails dug into the edge of a rough plank buried under the rubble. As he tore up the board, the pebbles on it dropped into the dark hole he'd uncovered, reverberating in the darkness below him as a whiff of stale air and the stench of mold clawed at his nostrils.

"It is here," Gompo whispered to the monks next to him, dropping back to his knees after handing the board to Amdma. Despite the cold air, the priest was covered with sweat. Ripping free another of the old planks, he cautiously lowered himself into the narrow pit, wondering how deep it was. His feet touched the bottom before he was below shoulder level. Feeling around the sides of the pit, he located a cavelike opening and ducked his head to step into a cavern beyond, feeling his way like a blind man because they couldn't risk producing any light.

After a quick conversation the monks above him snatched up the collection of torches they had fashioned of yak fat, rags, and sticks and lowered themselves into the opening to follow him. He cautiously traveled several meters into the blackness, his sandaled feet awkwardly navigating the rough floor.

As the passageway made an abrupt turn, Gompo halted. "Stop for a moment," he said to Amdma. "I'm going to light a torch." The old priest knelt and pulled flint and steel from his clothing. Then he felt for the oil-soaked end of his torch and held the steel against it. Rapidly tapping the stone against the metal, he produced a shower of sparks so bright that it almost hurt his eyes. He gently blew on the red embers of the torch, puffing tiny flames to life.

As the blaze grew, Amdma gasped. "Demons!" he moaned behind the old monk.

Gompo surveyed the cavern, holding up the torch to see better. He bit his lip and recognized what had frightened Amdma. Relaxing, he let go of the dagger he carried in his robes. "It's nothing to fear," he comforted the other monk. "Only the dead. Pass the word to those behind us."

He could hear Amdma swallow as he released the old priest's robe and turned to whisper to those beyond the bend in the tunnel, warning them of the fearful sight ahead.

The old monk shuffled on, musing over the striking diversity within the Buddhist faith, especially in the *mantrayana*, or "sacred recitation vehicle," forms of the religion that flourished in the Himalayan regions as well as in Mongolia and Japan.

The sects within the *mantrayana* believed in sacred dances and meditation; sex, they maintained, was designed for holy purposes.

But their beliefs in devils, goblins, and other deities often caused the splinter groups to diverge in their tenets as they tried to please various gods; many of the magic practices and rituals of each *sangha* were kept secret from outsiders, including surrounding Buddhist temples and other *sangha* communities.

*And such is certainly the case here*, he thought as he led the rescue party down the long tunnel he had discovered on the parchment drawing of the ancient citadel. The torch he carried flickered and seemed to cause the dusty mummies of the ancient monks lining the walls to shake and writhe in their niches.

*Buddhists outside Tibet cremate their dead*, the monk reflected, half awed by one of the crumbling figures he passed. In Tibet, however, cremation was restricted to the very wealthy because of the scarcity of wood and other flammable materials. The normal practice for most Buddhists was to sink bodies in the holy streams that flowed from the many mountains that made up the country. But water burial created other problems: The fish that ate the bodies often became contaminated and unfit for human consumption.

In areas without suitable streams or lakes, the people of Tibet practiced sky burial, slicing the body into bits and leaving the pieces out for the vultures to eat. This allowed the spirit to take flight with the birds, carrying the soul to heaven.

The earth burial practiced by the Chinese and most westerners caused Gompo to shudder. Since the earth was holy, putting bodies into it was a terrible sacrilege.

But the monks in the ancient citadel at Saga had

taken advantage of the cold, dry Tibetan climate to embalm and mummify their dead. That wasn't unheard of but was normally reserved for Buddhist saints. *That the small community at Saga had this many saints is unthinkable*, Gompo reasoned. So they had apparently been embalming most, perhaps all, of the monks in the monastery, possibly leaving the bodies for magic practices that could now only be guessed at since the Chinese had killed or scattered those of the original sect.

Behind him, Amdma brushed against one of the crumbling corpses and moaned again.

Gompo turned toward the cowering youth, noticing the arm that had broken off the mummified body; the limb swung back and forth, hanging on the rotten fabric of the corpse's robe. "We'll be past them soon," the old monk reassured Amdma. "Just watch my back and ignore the remains." Gompo stared past the youth down the line of wide-eyed monks who followed, carrying burning torches that flickered along the dark passageway. *If I were to yell*, he thought with a smile, *I could send the whole bunch of them stampeding back to the entrance of the tunnel.* What kind of a rescue party were they, anyway?

He unconsciously shook his head and turned back, continuing up the aisle of the dead, and remembered the time he had journeyed through a high, snow-filled mountain pass in his youth. He had discovered a party of five travelers on that trip, sitting around a campfire that had apparently burned out hours before.

"Run out of yak dung to burn?" he had asked, stamping the snow from his yak-leather boots before settling onto a cold rock next to the smallest of the strangers.

None of the wayfarers had answered. Pulling his fur cloak tightly around his thin frame, Gompo had studied the face of the man who sat across from him, the one who appeared to be staring at him rudely, eyes unblinking. "Am I not welcome here?" Gompo inquired of the traveler.

Still there had been no answer.

With sudden horror Gompo had realized that the five travelers had frozen to death, sitting around the fire that had finally burnt out, taking with it the lives of five people. Now they sat, seeming to stare at him, a light blanket of snow covering their purplish skins.

The cavern in which Gompo now found himself was warmer than the campsite had been, but he still experienced the eerie sense that lifeless eyes were rudely watching him as he journeyed past. *One has to wonder about the sanity of a* sangha *that constructed such a place,* he mused. Perhaps a demon had misled them.

"What is this?" he muttered to himself, holding his torch to the side and shading his eyes from its flickering yellow flame. Treading forward gingerly, he ran his hand over the wall in front of him. He had assumed that something like this must be ahead, but this appeared formidable. Now the question was whether they could deal with it or if their journey would come to an abrupt end without rescuing the Buddha.

The engines of the American helicopters popped in the nighttime air, creating a low-pitched, furious thumping that made it impossible to converse without the use of the aircraft's intercoms and radios.

Oz spoke over the radio, utilizing the short-range UHF battle-net channel. "BC Pack, this is Buddha's Crown One. Let's go by the numbers and see how we're doing."

The pilot of the lead AH-64 answered first. "Buddha's Crown Two is ready and waiting. Over."

"BC Three's up and running," the second Apache responded.

"BC Four is ready."

"BC Five is—on line now. Blew a relay but everything's okay."

Oz switched the radio to the CAN frequency and contacted the air boss on the USS *America* to receive flight clearance for the five helicopters. "This is Buddha's Crown One requesting permission to takeoff as per our flight plans."

"BC One, you are cleared for takeoff," the air boss radioed back. "We have your fuel bladders and the crews to mount them standing ready for your go-ahead."

Oz shifted back to the ABN frequency. "All right, boys, let's show these Navy wags how it's done. Two and Five, get into the air. But don't leave home without us—we need to pick up our fuel bladders. Once in the air, we'll hold a tight V formation."

The two AH-64s rose from the deck like angry insects, their dark shapes nearly invisible against the sky. They wheeled above the deck and headed out over the calm sea, waiting for the MH-60Ks to join them.

"BC One is going into a hover to pick up our fuel bladder—now," Oz called, lifting the collective pitch lever to boost the MH-60K into the air. He switched to his intercom. "How's it look back there, O.T.?"

"Flight crew's right on the ball," the warrant officer answered, leaning out his window. He watched as the small trucklike "mule" dragged a cart containing the huge black fuel bladder that would be attached to the carrying hook below the passenger compartment of the helicopter. Within seconds the bladder was in place, and the crew signaled the warrant officer. "We're all hooked up, Captain," O.T. called.

Oz lifted the chopper higher and pushed the control column, propelling the MH-60K out over the dark sea, dropping downward as it left the ground effect upblast from the deck. The pilot toggled his radio on. "All right, BC Three, move in and get your balloon."

Within minutes the remaining two MH-60Ks had picked up their fuel bladders, and all five American helicopters were flying in a wide V formation. Each pilot watched the "slimes" of the choppers beside him, judging the spacing for the formation by the faint position lights that were nearly invisible without the night-vision goggles the air crews wore.

The five helicopters switched to TF/TA radar and dropped closer to the ocean, nearly skimming it as they traveled in their tight formation. Oz switched his radio to Warner's command net frequency. "Mother Bird, Buddha's Crown One, Two, Three, Four, and Five are up and running. Over."

"BC One, you have a go-ahead for your mission," Warner's voice came back. "Silence, silence, silence," he finished, ordering them not to use the radio again unless there was an emergency.

The American choppers initiated their course across the Bay of Bengal off India. From there they would travel inland, hoping to avoid Chinese and Indian radar as they wove their way up the Jamuna River, raced through the narrow river valley of the Gangtok pass, and from there traveled toward their first LZ.

\* \* \*

Private Sung pulled his fur-lined hat down tighter over his ears as if that might somehow shut out the cold that seemed to ooze out of the darkness and fill his veins with frost. *Why do they have me watching this pass?* he wondered for the hundredth time that evening. He wished he had one of the new glow-in-the-dark watches with the red star in its center to tell what time it was; guard duty at night always seemed to stretch into eternity. But on his meager pay it would take a lifetime to earn one of the expensive timepieces. He settled down on the old barrel near the rock wall, resting his tired feet for a few moments.

Suddenly he started awake, the noise of a bull-dozer in his ears. *A bulldozer in the mountains?* he asked himself, shaking his head. He stood up and stamped his feet, realizing that he had fallen asleep on the barrel and had only been dreaming of his days on the earth-moving crew.

Napping on duty in the People's Army was fool-ish. If an officer caught a sleeping guard, it could mean paying a severe fine, and more than one guard who hadn't been caught had wound up with frost-bitten ears, nose, or fingers. With the poor medical treatment the army provided, that usually meant los-ing an appendage.

Wouldn't his wife like it if he came home to China without his nose. *I wonder why I dreamed of the old bulldozer?* he reflected. Then he heard the low thumping sound that had invaded his sleep. The wind shifted and blew up from the valley, carrying the pulsing fury of giant engines up the ridge. He strained his eyes, looking toward the noise, but saw nothing.

The throbbing became louder still, and abruptly the first of the machines slashed above his head, prompting the soldier to flatten himself against the ridge with an oath, his heart beating nearly as loudly as the blades above his head.

Just as he started to relax somewhat, another of the monsters shot overhead, blotting out the stars as he looked skyward. Then it, too, was gone. Rapidly it was followed by three more of the aircraft, and then the five vanished in the darkness above the ridge, with the reverberations of blades and engines rapidly becoming lost in the distance as they dropped behind the mountain.

With another oath Sung ripped off his fur cap and grabbed the headset of the telephone. Placing the device against his ear, oblivious to the cold metal and plastic against his skin, he cranked the handle on the body of the device and waited impatiently. Finally a voice on the other end answered.

"The Americans—five choppers—came through the pass just now," he reported, speaking rapidly in Chinese.

Silently he listened, then interrupted the soldier on the other end of the line. "Of course I'm sure—they nearly ripped my head off, they flew so low." He glanced at the stars and tried to remember in which direction the air machines had been headed when they had eclipsed the stars overhead. "They're headed northwest," he related. "Traveling very, very fast."

In a few minutes he repeated his story to an officer and was then ordered to hang up and renew his vigil. Replacing the headset onto its cradle, he grinned in the darkness, wondering if any more of the night fiends would hurtle overhead.

# 14

Gompo ran his hand over the rough obstruction that blocked the end of the passageway. "I knew it must be here," he told the other monks. "The *sangha* had to have hidden the end of the passageway that entered their monastery. Otherwise the Chinese would have destroyed the tunnel long ago."

"Can't we break through?" Targye asked, cautiously shoving against the surface of the plaster and stone. "It doesn't look very strong—see how it shakes."

"I'm sure we could," Gompo agreed. "But the Chinese would probably hear and be upon us before we even reached the hallway beyond, let alone the *bodhisattva*." He tapped the surface lightly with his knuckle. "It doesn't sound thick, but who knows?" The priest shook his head.

"Perhaps we can return tomorrow night with the proper tools," Targye suggested. "Our torches won't last much longer, and returning through the passageway in the dark . . ." He shivered, unable to finish the thought.

"May I take a look?" Amdma asked, squeezing

between the other two monks before either could answer. "I have an idea." As he reached out to touch the wall, he tripped over Targye's foot, falling head-long toward the barrier, his arms outstretched to break his fall.

As he fell into the facade, the wall crumbled away, spilling him headlong into the dark passage beyond in a riot of falling rock, plaster, and dust.

The three MH-60Ks and the two AH-64 gunships that accompanied them sped along on their roller-coaster ride over the mountains. As a mist rose into the night air, painted ghostly shades of white by the sliver of moon sinking behind the peaks along the western horizon, the shadows of the five aircraft danced above the uneven surface below, weaving in and out of the crevices like lost souls.

The stars overhead appeared brighter than before but twinkled less, because of the thin air, which also made the sky seem exceptionally black. Oz tugged his collar tighter to ward off the cold, which refused to be driven away even by the maxi-mum setting on the chopper's heater.

"We're about five clicks from our LZ at Phuntsogling," Death Song alerted the pilot.

"Great," Oz said. "I'm about worn out. Do you think—"

An alarm cut him off. Someone was bathing them with an invisible continuous-wave radar beam, targeting them in preparation for a missile launch. The pilot automatically triggered the radio switch on the control column. "Evasive action—scatter!" he ordered the convoy. "We've got bad guys. Arm your weapons and fire at will." He threw the helicopter out of formation.

"Death Song, give me the rockets and machine gun. Keep the Hellfires and countermeasures ready."

"Arming weapons."

All five American helicopters broke into rolls, putting distance between themselves as quickly as they could to create room to maneuver.

"Where are they?" Oz yelled, glancing over his shoulder.

"Coming up fast from six o'clock," Death Song replied.

*They're good,* the pilot thought grimly. They must have shadowed the American choppers and come in from behind without ever giving a hint of their presence until now. *And now it could be too late,* the pilot realized.

There was a flash from behind and to port, followed by a thunderclap that rumbled off the peaks.

Oz turned in his seat and glanced left; one of the Apaches tumbled through the air, its tail ripped off by a guided missile. As the aircraft plummeted, the fuel in its tanks ignited, turning it into a fireball before it reached the rocks below, where it fragmented into a hundred burning meteors. The pilot ignored the knot of anger in his stomach as he realized his buddies in the chopper were undoubtedly dead.

The victorious Chinese F-6 jet roared past the four remaining American helicopters, its cannon chattering as it fired another missile that chased the second Apache. The chopper released a cloud of chaff, confusing the sensors in the missile; the rocket flashed beyond the fleeing aircraft, crashed into a cliff, and exploded in a bright plume of fire and rock.

Oz shoved down on the collective pitch lever, plunging the helicopter downward so fast that he and his passengers hung weightless in their seat harnesses as they dropped over the edge of a cliff and plummeted down the mountainside toward the valley below.

As they passed the edge of the butte, the enemy radar warning ceased. "We're screened by the rock," Death Song explained, watching his screen for signs of other incoming jets. "Should we drop our fuel bladder?"

Oz considered the possibilities. If they dumped the fuel, it would effectively scrub the mission. But leaving the bladder slung below them would complicate his maneuvering to attack or escape from the Chinese jets. "Let's hang on to the bladder as long as we can," he finally answered.

Another barely discernible blip appeared on Death Song's scope. "We've got another bandit coming in over us!"

The Chinese jet dropped over the ridge behind them, following as they hurtled toward the valley floor and unleashing a volley of cannon fire that raised plumes of dirt ahead of them. As Oz threw the chopper to the side, the faster-moving jet pulled out of its dive, forced to climb to avoid smashing into the ground below.

The American pilot glanced upward and watched the Chinese jet roll over the peak beyond, preparing for another combat run at the enemy helicopter formation. Oz stopped the downward descent of the chopper, inducing him to regain his weight and then be smashed into his seat by g forces. The engines protested the abrupt stop, then checked the chopper's fall; he kicked his left pedal to follow the valley floor, fighting to keep control of the chopper as the fuel bladder sloshed below, rocking back and forth on its guy cable.

Shoving the chopper forward at maximum speed, he rapidly increased the space between the helicopter and the enemy jets, which were undoubtedly in pursuit. Then he toggled on his radio. "This is BC One. Anyone in a position to take these guys?"

The radio hissed. Then the voice of Lieutenant Welsh, the remaining Apache pilot, was heard. "You've got both of them circling around to come in on your tail, One. We can take the first one before it gets to you. But you're going to have to shake the second."

"Let's do it," Oz said, jerking the control column to change their course. While he couldn't outrun the incoming jets, he could outmaneuver them, rising and dropping faster than the Chinese aircraft.

Bright tracers arced over them, announcing the presence of the planes on their tail. The projectiles passed, scouring the ground the chopper would have traversed if the pilot had not altered their course.

As the night sky lit up behind them, Oz assumed one of the jets on his tail had fired a missile, but the radar indicated no continuous-wave beam. Instead, the radio crackled to life as Welsh called from BC Three: "Our Hellfire is off. Hang on, One, the second jet's jockeying to cut you off on your present course."

The fire-and-forget Hellfire missile from the AH-64 quickly accelerated to Mach 1.17 as it chased after the lead F-6, targeted by the nose laser controlled by the gunner in the chopper. The Schmidt-Cassegrain telescope in the nose of the Hellfire locked its microprocessor logic circuit onto the image of the jet and tracked it.

Apparently unaware of the missile pursuing him, the pilot of the jet slowed to bank, following Oz as he changed to another heading. As the plane reduced its speed, the oncoming Hellfire automatically altered its course to home closer to the target, catching up to the Chinese jet and detonating upon impact. Secondary explosions of the plane's missiles and fuel tank split the plane apart as it tumbled toward the earth.

"One, this is Three," Welsh called from the Apache. "We've got the second bastard in our sights—" There was static, and then the Apache pilot resumed. "Hang on. There're two more jets coming in. Over."

"Where are they?" Oz asked.

"They're on our tail," Welsh called frantically. "We're going to have to—"

A bright light flashed over the valley, and then another explosion rocked the MH-60K. "Is that the second jet?" Oz interrogated his crew, craning around in his seat to see what was behind him. "Come in, Three."

"One, this is Four. There're two more jets— Three's down. The other's on our tail now. We can't seem to shake it!"

There was another massive explosion, and the radio was silent.

Death Song glanced up from his radar. "The third jet's overshooting us—looks clear."

"Damn those Chinese bastards!" Oz hissed. "Let's see if we can set this fuel bladder down without breaking it." He lowered the chopper toward the earth, then pulled into a hover, lowering them almost to the rocky terrain before reaching forward on the control column to trigger the black release lever. The fuel bladder dropped the short distance, freeing the chopper to lift skyward.

"Another jet's coming in on our tail, pinging us!" Death Song yelled over the sound of the radar warning buzzer.

Oz yanked the column to the right, throwing the aircraft into a banking turn as the Chinese jet neared them, its cannon blazing. The plane failed to compensate quickly enough for the chopper's new course heading, and the tracer projectiles flashed past the Americans.

"Everybody hang on," Oz warned as the jet pulled onto the chopper's new heading. "I'm going to try a tree topper." Oz kicked the rudder pedals as he flexed the control column, maintaining their speed as the chopper rotated about its axis. Abruptly the helicopter was flying backward, nose up, facing the oncoming jet.

Aiming the chopper's nose directly toward the F-6, he hit the fire button of his rocket launcher, sending three unguided rockets toward the oncoming Chinese plane.

At nearly the same instant the F-6 pilot fired his cannon; as its muzzle flashed, Oz felt as if he were looking right down its bore. He swung the helicopter through another tree-topper turn, and the projectiles flashed past the chopper, missing the cabin by only three feet. He banked again, racing at right angles away from the path of the oncoming jet.

One of the American missiles exploded as the jet's cannon hit the 2.75-inch rocket accelerating toward it. The second unguided missile continued harmlessly past the F-6, but the third struck the intake port of the jet's engine, instantly rending the plane apart with its explosive and igniting the fuel. The secondary detonation transformed the jet into a tumbling fireball, propelled forward by the momentum of the wreckage.

A curse escaped Oz's lips as he realized the jet pilot had altered course moments before the rocket had connected with his plane. Now the fiery wreckage was headed straight for the MH-60K. The American pilot frantically slammed the control column to the side, attempting to avoid the inferno that was toppling toward him, lighting the sky as it descended.

The debris was nearly overhead when Oz succeeded in avoiding the worst of it, but bits of molten metal showered the Americans as it flashed past, shattering across the boulders below.

The chopper began to shake with each rotation of its blades. "Rotor imbalance," Oz yelled, holding tightly to the control column vibrating in his hands. "Some of the debris must have damaged the rotors."

"Third jet's coming in from two o'clock," Death Song cautioned. "It's locking on to us!" The warning beeper alerted them to the F-6's continuous-wave radar, which delineated them to the semiactive homing guidance system on the Type 91 missile.

The pilot maneuvered toward the left, searching the area from where he knew the plane must be approaching. A moment later he spotted it, its wings lit by the flash and smoke of the Type 91 missile it had launched.

"Missile!" Oz warned his crew as he raised the collective pitch lever, attempting to gain some altitude. Shoving the shaking control column forward, he increased their speed. As it accelerated, the chopper threatened to shake itself apart, but the vibration finally ceased as the blades increased their speed.

Death Song released a flare and chaff from the countermeasures pod, hoping one or both would confuse the oncoming rocket. "I've activated our countermeasures," he reported.

As the MH-60K cleared a cliff, Oz lowered the collective pitch lever, dropping them toward the river far below; the tail rotors nearly collided with the stone facade, the echo of the rotors booming off the rock face as they swooped downward.

The guidance system of the rocket ignored the flare, speeding past the bright device that sputtered on its tiny parachute. When the Type 91 missile sliced into the cloud of metal foil released from the chopper's countermeasures pod, the chaff scattered the radar reflections from the jet into a kaleidoscope of electronic patterns, prompting the missile to chase the various electronic shadows reflected from the bits of aluminum. Sensing that it had lost its intended target, the missile's electronic circuits exploded its warhead in a brilliant flash.

The F-6 that was tailing the helicopter cleared the cliff and dived after its prey, firing another Type 91 missile; Oz pulled up and turned to follow the narrow canyon carved out of the rock by the stream that flowed below.

The missile failed to track its target as the chopper progressed along the jagged environment. Self-destructing, the warhead rocked the night with its blast. Because it was unable to slow without stalling, the jet pulled out of its dive and overshot the helicopter, climbing upward to bank for another attack run.

"Let's take him with a Hellfire!" Oz yelled, lifting

the helicopter out of the canyon and chasing after the retreating jet. He shoved the control column forward, increasing his speed to the maximum and hoping the damaged rotors would stay together. For four long seconds the blades vibrated perilously; then they settled into their increased speed without further quivering.

Death Song turned his head slowly, giving the FLIR targeting system time to follow his movement. Centering the jet in the aiming monocle attached to his helmet, he activated the laser target designator. "I've got him in my sights! Launching Hellfire," he announced.

The missile dropped from its pylon and blossomed to life, shooting ahead of the MH-60K on its tail of fire. The rocket seemed to be losing the race against the jet until the Chinese pilot realized he was under attack. Banking sharply, he tried to shake the Hellfire, but the maneuver only brought the missile closer as it jockeyed into a new angle of approach that cut the distance between it and the aircraft.

In another second the missile caught up, colliding with the jet's tail and ripping it apart in a massive explosion that turned the aircraft into metal confetti.

"One, this is Five. You've got another jet on your tail," the radio crackled. "Dive! We'll try to get him into our sights."

Oz threw the helicopter downward toward the canyon below, again suspending the crew and passengers in their shoulder harnesses as the MH-60K fell earthward. The warning buzzer alerted them to enemy radar; the jet was targeting them with a missile.

As the chopper continued its plunge, the pilot slowly raised the collective pitch lever to check their fall, careful not to decelerate too quickly and present an easy target. He shoved the control column to the side to negotiate the tight bend of the river ahead.

"The jet still hasn't launched," O.T. called from the back.

"He's having trouble with his radar," Death Song said. "But it's coming back on now."

"Hang on," the radio crackled in Oz's ears. "We've got him in our sights!" called the pilot of Buddha's Crown Five.

The boulders below the MH-60K flashed with the telltale reflection of a missile launch. *Is that the Hellfire or the Chinese missile?* Oz wondered. "Anybody see who launched that missile?" he called over the intercom.

"It's the Hellfire!" O.T. reported from the gunner's compartment. "The jet still hasn't launched."

*You're headed in too fast,* Oz warned himself as the ground rushed up to meet him. Instinctively he jerked up on the collective pitch lever, slowing the MH-60K; again its rotors vibrated, this time so violently that he nearly lost his grip on the control column. "Death Song, be ready to grab the stick. I'm not sure I can hold it."

"I'm ready to assist," the copilot promised.

*Hope this crate holds together,* Oz thought grimly, pushing the chopper past the face of a huge granite boulder and following the streambed. Suddenly a bright flash lit the sky, and within seconds the noise of the concussion reverberated along the canyon walls, shaking the chopper. "Did Five get the jet?" Oz asked over the intercom. "Did anyone see?"

"The jet's at three o'clock," Luger called from behind Death Song. "Five got him but didn't do much damage. Looks like he might still pull out."

Oz glanced out his side window and saw the jet tumbling earthward, its left wing tip torn away by the missile. As the F-6 continued to fall, the Chinese pilot tried desperately to regain control, but the unmanageable aircraft smashed into the mountainside. The explosion rattled the night as the fireball climbed skyward, rapidly changing into a thick cloud of smoke.

"This is Five," the voice of Lieutenant Sam Jackson called over the radio. "That's the last jet," he reported, "but they managed to knock out Two, Three, and Four. One of their shells hit inside our passenger compartment. At least four of my dogs are dead; the medic says the others are all suffering from wounds—some minor and four major."

"How much damage to your chopper?"

"Negligible," Jackson replied. "Our instruments show minor damage only."

"We need to pick up any survivors from the downed birds," Oz instructed, turning his chopper and climbing skyward. "Did you see where they crashed?"

"We saw all three hits," Jackson answered. "But I don't think we're going to find any survivors. The secondary detonations were lethal. Over."

Oz swallowed hard and held the control column tightly as it again started vibrating uncontrollably. Finally he spoke. "Five, you circle and provide cover while I scan the wreckage. We're not leaving until we're certain there're no survivors. Then we'll go back so the medics can handle your wounded."

# 15

Gompo stepped out into the dark hallway to recover Amdma, steeling himself for the gunfire that he knew would erupt at any moment. The old priest held his torch high above his head in the cold stone hallway, glancing up and down the passageway. Nothing.

He reached down and grabbed Amdma's hand, helping the young monk to his feet as bits of plaster and stone crunched under his sandals.

"You fool!" Targye whispered, hissing like a snake. "We'll have to leave now. The Chinese guards will be on top of us any minute. Come on!"

"Perhaps not," Gompo dissented, eyes darting up and down the passageway. There was no light except from the torches the monks carried.

"Perhaps the *bodhisattva* has made them deaf," Amdma suggested, brushing the dust from his robe. He picked up the torch he'd dropped and touched it to Gompo's, relighting it.

"We're far below ground here," the old priest maintained. "Perhaps the Chinese aren't using this section of the citadel. They don't have a large garrison here in Saga."

"The *bodhisattva* has made them deaf," Amdma repeated, oblivious to the old monk's explanation.

"Perhaps," Targye said, speaking softly as if he believed the Chinese were listening. "But I still think we should go back and try again tomorrow. What if someone did hear you and went for reinforcements? They could be back any minute."

"Let me see the map," Gompo said to the monk entrusted with the parchment.

He handed it to Gompo, who knelt on the rough stones, spread the map flat on the uneven floor, and held his flickering torch up to it.

The priests were quiet, their eyes catching the torchlight. Gompo wondered if they thought he was foolishly obsessed with taking them farther into the dangerous prison. But they had to find the Buddha.

The old monk tapped the diagram with a gnarled finger. "We're here," he said. "Let's continue on—down this passageway here to our left." He pointed. Rising to his feet, he handed the sketch back and spoke. "Our Dalai Lama is that way. We must go to free the Buddha. Targye, carve marks in the walls as we proceed so the rest of you can find your way back if something happens to me or the map." Without waiting to see if they followed, the old monk set out down the hallway, his sandals echoing into the darkness ahead.

At first the priests stood speechless, unsure of their course of action. Then, as Amdma hurried after the old man, the others quickly followed. Targye reached out with his knife and slashed an X onto the rock, then turned to bring up the rear.

*   *   *

Landing and checking the burning wreckage, Oz discovered no survivors in any of the choppers downed by the F-6s. After Oz set his chopper down and O.T. refastened the fuel tank to the underside of the MH-60K, he reluctantly left the crash sites, leaving behind the burnt bodies of the American soldiers.

Although he knew he would want his men to complete their mission if anything happened to him, he still felt guilty about leaving the corpses behind.

As he proceeded toward the LZ, which he hoped was far enough from the site of the air battle to avoid detection, the chopper seemed to shudder, rocking the whole frame of the aircraft. *This crate's not likely to go much farther than the LZ,* he thought, tightening his grip on the control column.

The rotors felt unbalanced, convincing him that it would only be a matter of time before the severe vibrations damaged the drive shaft or the blades or jarred some of the delicate electronic modules loose inside the cabin. The bottom line was they'd have to land soon to make repairs, perhaps even abandon the aircraft. He pushed the thought from his mind; being stranded inside Tibet was not his idea of a good time.

"We're nearly there," Death Song announced, glancing up from the HSD screen.

"That ridge straight ahead?" the pilot asked.

"That's it."

Within seconds Oz had circled the ruins of the abandoned lamasery near Phuntsogling. A tall castle-like structure jutted from the tallest of the cliffs, and the vestiges of a tiny village surrounded the hillside. During his briefing Oz had learned that the Chinese had destroyed the village in 1965 after an informant had betrayed the monks, who taught that the state was second to Buddha.

The priests were rounded up, and their religious leaders killed. The rest of the order was tortured and exiled from the village by the Chinese, who then dynamited the major buildings, leaving ruins where a thriving community had once stood. But a few of the roofless structures remained standing, their heavy brick walls still capable of concealing the two American choppers that circled overhead.

"BC Five," Oz called to the MH-60K pilot flying behind him, "we'll set down inside the largest ruins to the south. There's enough room to accommodate both our copters. That should make us pretty hard to see from the air."

"That's a roger, One. We'll follow you in."

"I wish we could continue our mission," Oz told his crew over the intercom. "But we've got to see if we can get our chopper repaired before we shake ourselves apart."

The two pilots carefully set their fuel bladders in the dark ruins at the summit of the hill; then the helicopters settled toward the earth, hovering over the rubble before slowly sinking into it, the blades of the rotors stirring storms of dust as they descended into the ravaged remains of the village.

"Sudden, better get some men out to keep a watch," Oz called over the intercom to the Delta Force lieutenant in the passenger compartment behind him. "I don't know how long we'll be here on the ground."

"I've got the teams ready to go," the black officer answered. "How bad's the damage? It felt like you were using the blades to scramble eggs back here."

"We won't know how bad it is until we take a look at it," the pilot replied, setting the engines to idle as he and Death Song began to shut down the aircraft. "If it's a rotor tracking problem, we may be up the creek without a paddle. I'm hoping it's just some minor damage to the blades, but it sure doesn't feel like it."

The Delta Force guards scrambled through the side doors of the MH-60K as the pilot and copilot quickly shut down the noisy twin engines; the turbine-powered rotors spun to a stop, leaving only the high-pitched whine of the auxiliary power unit.

"Better link us to Commander Warner," Oz told Death Song, releasing the control column and shaking his gloved hand to get the cramp out of it.

Within minutes the copilot had uplinked the MH-60K's communications computer to the COMSAT overhead, and their radio signals were relayed back to the USS *America,* which was still positioned in the Indian Ocean. Oz quickly explained to Warner that three of the five aircraft in the convoy had been lost in the Chinese ambush. "That's where we now stand," the pilot finished, after describing their mechanical difficulties.

"I don't see how they could have known where you were headed," Warner told the pilot. "Agent Chung couldn't have given your precise entrance even if he got caught by the Chinese, since he didn't have the information. But it's possible the presence of a foreign agent in the area alerted them to have spotters ready. Someone on the ground must have observed you, and the Chinese were able to scramble their jets in time to cut you off before you got past them."

"Enough bad luck to last a lifetime."

"I'd say so," Warner agreed. "I'll have to check

with Washington to see if they want you to go ahead, but I know they'll ask how you feel about it. Do you want to scrub the mission?"

"Let me assess the damage to our chopper first," Oz responded. "If it's minor, we might be able to continue. We still have most of our armament and the Delta Force squad. Both our fuel bladders survived the battle, so we'll still have both choppers if we can get our problem fixed."

"All right, then. Check the aircraft and get back to me ASAP. In the meantime I'll let Washington know what's happened—they may nix it on their end. Damn, I wish Sergeant Marvin were there to check out the damage."

"He could probably bail us out if anyone could. But he's not here, so we'll have to see what we can do on our own. I'll get back to you ASAP."

"I'll be waiting. Over and out."

After the chopper's APU was shut down, the crew of the damaged MH-60K climbed onto the top of the fuselage and carefully inspected the helicopter in the darkness, utilizing their AN/PVS-6 night-vision goggles and L-shaped Army flashlights, positioning a red lens over each bulb to minimize the chances of being detected.

"I can't see anything wrong with the lead-lag struts," Luger said.

"If there was a problem with them, we probably wouldn't be here." O.T. laughed.

"Yeah, guess that's right," Luger agreed. "The chopper would have shook itself apart when we landed."

"Go ahead and check everything," Oz told his crew. "Even if it's something like lead-lag struts, we don't want to miss anything that might be damaged."

"Just what I was doing, Captain," Luger said sheepishly.

"I think I found our problem," Death Song declared, tapping one of the titanium and fiberglass rotor blades. He pointed toward the forward end of the blade, which extended beyond the front of the chopper. "Look out there."

The other three crewmen studied the spot where he had pointed. A footlong chunk of the leading edge of the blade was missing, apparently torn off by the debris that had hit the chopper.

"That looks like the problem, all right," Oz agreed. "Let's give everything else the once-over just to be sure. Then I'll get back to Warner."

"I wish Sergeant Marvin were here," O.T. said.

Oz rubbed his chin. "You know, that gives me an idea."

"Night demons," Norbu's wizened uncle Bobolanga whispered, fearful the monsters on the plain below them might overhear.

"No, Uncle," Norbu replied. "Those are only sky cars with men inside."

"But they hover in the air like hummingbirds," the old man protested. "They must be demons."

"No. They are like the machines the Chinese used to kill our people in Lhasa before they took the Buddha."

"Worse than demons, then," Bobolanga said. "But what are the Chinese doing in the ruins of the Phuntsogling lamasery? Aren't they satisfied with having destroyed it once?"

"Perhaps they're searching for the Buddha—the monks should have him free by now," suggested another of the rebels on the ridge, his voice materializing out of the darkness.

Norbu picked with a fingernail at a rust spot on the old flintlock he held. "One thing's for certain," he mused. "If they find the meeting place tomorrow, when the Dalai Lama gets there, they'll take him again or even kill him this time."

"And destroy everyone there while they're at it," Bobolanga added glumly, pulling his fur hat down over his ears to ward off the cold night air.

"Perhaps we were kept from reaching the meeting place for a reason," Norbu said, rising to his feet. He took a deep breath and invoked the ancient greeting that had become their rallying cry. "*Om Mani Padme Hum*—Hail to the Jewel in the Lotus."

"*Om Mani Padme Hum*," a chorus of voices answered from the darkness around him.

"If we can't reach the meeting place," he told the gathering, "perhaps we can still surprise the heathen communists in the dark and destroy them for our Buddha. And *now* is the time to attack the Chinese, while they sit in the valley below. The gods have put them at our feet for us to destroy."

"The Chinese will exterminate us if those are the same machines that killed so many at Lhasa," a voice protested from the darkness.

"No," another argued. "Norbu is right. They must not be aware of our presence; otherwise they would have attacked—or never have landed where we could see them."

"That's my thinking," Norbu said. "This is the time to hit them. And if we destroy the helicopters, there'll be two less of the savage machines for the murderers to fight us with later."

No one else spoke.

"What do you say?" Norbu asked. "Will we take advantage of the luck that has fallen into our laps?"

"Perhaps you're right," Bobolanga said.

"Let's go," called one of the disembodied voices on the hillside. Others muttered agreement.

Norbu glanced down the slope toward the spot where they had seen the aircraft vanish into the ruins. "Let us destroy the Chinese helicopters that desecrate the holy places of our land. Victory to the gods."

"Victory to the gods," the voices answered.

In a matter of minutes Norbu and the others had made their simple plans for the surprise attack in whispers and low murmurs. A quarter of an hour later the twenty-five rebels began their descent of the winding trail down the slope, traveling slowly to feel out the path in the darkness. They picked their way toward the village below, rifles cocked, ready to slay the enemies whom the gods had delivered at their feet.

# 16

Gompo led the way through the winding, pitch-black hallway in the bowels of the citadel. His fellow monks followed behind, each clinging to the robe of the priest ahead of him like a string of blind beggars. The old man leading the parade held his knife tight in his hand, ready to attack any being or demon he chanced to meet in the darkness.

*The trick,* Gompo told himself, *will be getting to the prison cells.* That area would be heavily guarded, and stealing past the guards would be a miraculous feat if they could somehow accomplish it. *But getting this far is a miracle in itself,* he reflected.

The monk slowed his pace, and Amdma, following closely behind as if fearful that a devil might pluck him away from the others, bumped into him. Gompo ignored the young priest and studied the hallway up ahead. Yes, it was getting lighter, but was that a sign of danger?

There was only one way to find out.

He continued on, slowly nearing the bright spot that might be only an optical illusion in the darkness. In a few minutes he realized he was nearing a corner.

Gingerly rounding the bend, he searched up and down the intersecting passageway. A bright spot lit the passageway far ahead of him where another hall converged with his own. Though he didn't wish to do so, he turned and headed for the light. That was the path that would take them to the Dalai Lama.

He made his way carefully down the hallway, which was formed of hand-hewn stones held in place with crumbling mortar; trailing behind him was the procession of monks, who now proceeded gingerly with their knives drawn. Little by little the light grew brighter until Gompo's eyes began to water, accustomed as they were to the pitch black.

Nearing the intersection of the crumbling corridors, he again slowed his pace, finally halting before crossing into the light. Pressing his back against the wall, he took a deep breath and peered around the corner.

In the lighted hallway beyond, a guard squatted with his back against the stone wall and his eyes closed, smoking a long wooden pipe. His rifle was cradled across his knees.

Gompo jerked his head back into the darkness before the Chinese soldier could spot him.

"What is it?" Amdma whispered, his voice reverberating up and down the halls.

The old monk turned and shushed the young man before he could say more, but it was too late. The guard's voice echoed along the hallway. "Who's here?" he demanded, his rifle scraping against the stones as he rose to his feet. "Who is down here with me?" he bellowed. "Ting Hung, is that you? You'd better not be playing another trick on me. I'm tired of these games, and I will report you."

The soldier's leather boots scraped along the floor, and the long spike bayonet on his rifle extended into the darkness around the corner, just inches from Gompo's face. "Who's there?" he demanded again, probing the darkness. The bayonet, frozen in place a moment, began to inch forward, followed by the stock. Finally the soldier leaned into the passageway, attempting to see into the dimness beyond.

Before the guard could react, Gompo jabbed his knife into his chest; jerking the blade out, he slashed it across the man's throat. The soldier tried to scream, but only a bubbling groan escaped his lips.

Amdma leaped past the old priest, clutching at the rifle the soldier was attempting to bring into play. Gompo slashed across the trooper's spine as the young monk dragged their opponent to the floor. Another slash cut through the guard's vertebrae, abruptly inducing him to lose consciousness as a pool of blood formed around him on the stony floor.

"Let me have the rifle," Amdma cried, elbowing the other monks who ringed the fallen soldier and seizing it.

"No," Targye asserted. "I am the rifleman of our group. I know the most about these tools of death."

Amdma held the bloody weapon to his chest, refusing to let it go.

Gompo wiped his blade clean on the green uniform of the guard and then glanced up. "Let Amdma keep it," he instructed. "We must use our knives if we're not to attract attention. Now come this way—we have no time to lose."

Targye glared at the young monk clutching the

rifle, then turned and slashed another X onto the stone wall.

* * *

As Amdma and the others followed Gompo down the narrow passageway, they were amazed at the speed the old man attained, his red robes flapping around him, his sandals clicking lightly on the rock. Finally the old monk slowed down, rounded a corner, and started up a set of narrow stairs.

*Does this old fool really know where he's headed?* Amdma asked himself. They'd be lucky if he didn't get them all killed. *Of course that would solve a few problems,* the young monk thought, clutching the rifle a bit tighter. *The trick will be keeping the Chinese from killing me along with the others.* If only he had been able to contact Major Ling to inform him of their plans. But there had been no way with the other monks present day and night.

The column of monks slowed as Gompo downed another of the guards, instantly dispatching the man with a brutal cut to the back of the neck. *Gompo should have been a butcher,* Amdma snickered to himself, wincing at the sight of the blood collecting around the remains.

Again they jogged down the hall, following the old monk, who seemed to fly almost like a fiend. *If their luck holds up, they will succeed in reaching the Buddha,* the young monk fretted.

*That leaves only one thing to do.*

Amdma slowed his pace until the others had passed. Then he stopped, flipped the safety off his rifle, and knelt. After he took careful aim at the

backs of the monks ahead of him, his finger rapidly
pumped the trigger, downing two of the priests
with his first shots. Quickly he pulled the trigger
again and again, killing all but Gompo and one other
man, who dashed around the corner ahead of him.

The young monk threw the empty rifle to the
ground and raised his hands above his head, waiting for
the Chinese guards, who he knew would arrive soon.

Within seconds he heard the scraping of heavy
combat boots on the stone floor as four Chinese soldiers in wrinkled green uniforms appeared in the
hallway ahead of him. The troopers gaped at the fall-
en bodies of the monks littering the hall, then at the
priest standing in front of them in his red robe,
hands in the air.

"What's going on?" one of the soldiers quizzed
his companions.

"I killed them," Amdma answered the man in
perfect Chinese. "Now take me to Major Ling. I have
an important message for him."

The soldier stood motionless, unsure what to do.

"I am the informant who works for Major Ling,"
the priest declared, lowering his arms. "Take me to
him at once or he'll have your head."

The trooper swallowed hard, blinking in surprise. "Get your hands back over your head," he said
finally. "I'll take you to him. But don't try anything."

"It was Amdma," Targye gasped, panting for
breath as he rushed along behind Gompo. "I saw
him before we rounded the corner. He shot the others, the traitor!"

"Shhhh," the older monk hissed. He stopped

and thrust himself against the wall, his bony hand shoving Targye into the nook beside him. "Quiet!"

The heavy tramp of booted feet came closer, and a squad of Chinese soldiers sprinted past, headed for the area where the shooting had just occurred.

Targye let out his breath in a rattling hiss.

"For now we must concentrate on getting the *bodhisattva*," the old monk whispered. "We will worry about why Amdma did what he did later."

"Yes, of course." Targye nodded, nostrils flaring as he caught his breath. "We must free the Buddha." He quickly surveyed the passageway. "Everything looks clear."

Gompo leapt out of their hiding place like a rabbit and hurried toward another flight of stairs, with Targye tagging along behind, totally confused by the winding passageways. *I sure hope Gompo knows where he's going,* he thought, jogging along behind the surefooted old monk and trying to steel himself for the rifle fire he assumed was imminent.

But the gunfire never came. The two monks ascended the flight of rough stone steps and plastered themselves against the wall in the narrow hallway beyond.

"The Dalai Lama's cell should be around the corner at the end of this long hallway—if the map was correct," Gompo told the other monk breathlessly.

*If,* Targye thought. By all the gods in heaven he hoped the map and Gompo's memory were correct. His fear was so tangible, he felt he could almost wrap his fingers around it, as if it were leaking from every pore in his skin.

He forced himself to pay attention to Gompo as the old man leaned over, whispering in his ear. "No matter what happens to me, I want you to continue on and free the *bodhisattva*. Do you understand?"

"Nothing is going to happen to you that doesn't happen to me," Targye whispered back.

"Let's go." Gompo straightened his skinny frame and peered around the corner, dodging the point of a bayonet that unexpectedly jabbed at him. With lightning speed the old man sliced the soldier's throat as he stepped out of the darkness.

The guard dropped to his knees, seizing his throat in an effort to stanch the flood of blood; the blade in Gompo's hand cut into his back, severing his spine and paralyzing him instantly. The man sprawled onto the stone floor.

Targye scooped up the fallen man's rifle, attempting to ignore the soldier's eyes, which gaped up at him. He fumbled at the safety, releasing it finally, then turned to follow Gompo, who was running up ahead.

"What's going on in here?" a husky Chinese voice demanded from behind the priests. "Halt!"

Without thinking, Targye whirled around in a flurry of red robes and steel and fired. The thundering report of his weapon made him blink as the .30-caliber bullet exploded out of the muzzle.

Instantly he opened his eyes and beheld the uninjured guard charging toward him, drawing his holstered Mauser pistol as he came.

The priest's second shot connected with the target as the Chinese sergeant clutched his chest and tumbled to the floor, his pistol pirouetting over the stones and coming to rest at Targye's feet.

Before the monk could catch his breath, another soldier appeared, firing his Type 79 submachine gun and sending a stream of bullets smashing along the wall in front of Targye. The projectiles tore chips of rock from the wall, stinging the monk's face; the heavy slugs hummed like angry bees as they ricocheted past his head.

The priest's skill with a rifle returned to him. Aiming his weapon and tapping the trigger, he released a blast that raised a thin blue cloud of smoke in front of him.

A third bloody eye appeared in the guard's forehead as if by magic, reminding the monk of an ancient painting of a three-eyed demon. The Chinese officer toppled over, and abruptly everything was quiet except for the priest's tortured breathing.

"Come on!" Gompo hissed from up ahead.

Targye turned to see the old man standing in the corridor waiting impatiently for him. But Targye's eyes fastened on his elderly comrade for only a moment before discerning the two figures who stood beyond the priest, covering the monks with shouldered rifles, ready to shoot.

Without thinking, Targye raised his own weapon to fire.

# 17

"So the mission's scrubbed?" Death Song inquired.

"Yeah." Oz nodded, standing with the hot mug of coffee O.T. had handed him. The other three crewmen sat around a small stove, boiling a pan of water to take a little of the edge off the frosty night air. A large camouflage net hid the flame from the air, while the walls of the old building kept the cold wind out.

"Nobody seems to know where Sergeant Marvin is," Oz informed them. "I'll check back with Commander Warner in about half an hour to find out if we can make the repairs on our own," he added. "Washington thinks we have too few Delta Force troops to pull off a rescue, and they're probably right. In the meantime, Marvin's assistant thinks we can get the blades balanced with tape so the chopper will be ready for the trip back to the *America*."

"Tape?" Luger asked.

"Yeah." Oz nodded. "If we get the right number of wraps in the right place, we can balance out the blades. We'll start the repair work in a little while."

"It's possible to repair a blade with tape?" the gunner asked incredulously.

"We did it all the time in Nam." O.T. laughed. "The tape just supplies the weight to balance things out. It doesn't need to hold anything together—just needs to hang on for the ride."

"It works," Oz reassured Luger. "The question is how many wraps of tape and where. But I'm hoping Sergeant Marvin can help us figure that out over the COMSAT."

"Just like the old Hueys we flew." O.T. grinned. "Half the time those babies were held together with baling wire and bubble gum."

Luger shook his head. "I never thought I'd be flying in a chopper held together with duct tape."

"It beats walking," Death Song added dryly.

"Yeah," Luger agreed. "I guess it'd be one hell of a walk to the Tibetan border."

"Thanks for the coffee," Oz said, handing his empty tin mug back to O.T. "I'm going to check with the medic again to see how the wounded are doing. Hopefully they'll locate Sergeant Marvin before long so he can help us figure out where to position the tape. In the meantime, you three finish checking out the helicopter."

"Yes, sir," the three crewmen answered almost in unison.

"That should do it," Marvin's voice crackled over the radio connected to the helicopter's satellite link.

"I hope so," Oz replied, completing what he hoped was the final wrap of green duct tape on the rotor.

"Be sure all the edges are smoothed down," Marvin instructed the pilot. "Otherwise moisture can get under the tape. That wouldn't bother the adhesive—it's waterproof. But it could change the weight enough to throw the balance off, and it could form ice, which will gradually work the tape loose."

"Will do," Oz replied, carefully slicing a strip of tape off the roll with the serrated blade of a Spyderco Clipit. He folded the knife and then smoothed the tape down, ensuring that it adhered tightly to the rotor blade. "It looks tight," he reported to Marvin. "Not as good as you'd do, but I think it'll hold."

"Sounds like you did okay—for a ham-handed pilot," Marvin joshed him. "I know you're tired of testing the rotors, but if you have time, you should start her up once more just to be sure."

"Okay, we'll do it. If we run into problems, we'll get in touch; otherwise I'm hoping we won't need to talk to you until we get back."

"Sounds good," Marvin agreed. "Guess we better sign off so we don't run up Uncle Sugar's phone bill. Good luck to you."

"Thanks," Oz answered. "Over and out." The pilot switched off the radio and replaced it in his belt pouch. Inspecting his work once more, he rubbed at a wrinkle in the tape, then carefully descended from the top of the chopper.

"How's it look?" O.T. asked.

"It looks good," the pilot reported, handing the warrant officer the roll of tape to store in the tool kit inside the helicopter. "The proof will be whether or not it works."

Oz unlatched his door and climbed into the pilot's seat. "Looks like we need to start it one more time to check for vibrations," he told Death Song.

"This is worse than flight training school," the copilot deadpanned.

"I think this should be the last test," Oz told him. "But I want to be sure the rotors are perfectly stabilized before we head out."

Within minutes the two crewmen had the engines up to speed and the rotors at the RPM that had given them difficulties. "Looks like we have it whipped for now," Oz finally said, easing up on the throttle. "Let's shut it down and hope the tape hangs on till we get home."

As Oz stepped out of the cabin, rubbing the stubble on his chin, he wondered if there was any way they could have continued the mission, since the damage to the MH-60K had proved to be only minor. The repairs on the helicopter would make it possible to complete the assignment, but the number of injured Delta Force troops in the remaining helicopter would pose a problem.

No, Washington was probably right; the remaining squad of soldiers might be sufficient to carry out the assault on the Chinese citadel *if* nothing else went wrong. But that was too big a gamble on a military mission like this one.

"Captain Carson."

The pilot turned around. "Sudden?"

"Excuse me, sir, but we've got what looks like some soldiers headed our way—coming down that ridge overlooking our position."

"Why would the Chinese have a patrol in such a desolate area?" Oz asked.

"I don't know, sir," the lieutenant answered, motioning the pilot over to the small radar assembly half hidden in the corner of the open, barnlike building where the chopper was concealed. "I can't imagine they'd have men on foot searching for us yet, even if they have managed to pinpoint our position."

"Which they don't seem to have done, judging from the air traffic," Oz remarked, slipping under the camouflage netting that shielded the portable radar assembly the Delta Force had set up.

"But there's definitely movement on that hill," Sudden declared, tapping the glowing green screen in front of the radar operator.

"How large a force?" the pilot asked the technician.

"Looks like thirty men, sir. All armed, judging from the heavy pings."

"But why are they trying to get so close?" Oz asked. "The Chinese would normally use mortars if they knew we were down here."

"That's exactly what I was thinking." Sudden nodded. "Maybe they're out without a radio and are just coming in to investigate."

"I wonder if they could be Tibetans," Oz mused.

"No way to tell with this equipment," the radar operator interjected.

"But I don't see why any Tibetans would be sneaking up on us like this," Sudden stewed. "We've got our high-power binocs set up on the wall above here if you want to take a look."

"Let's see what they look like," the pilot said.

The two officers scrabbled up the crumbling mud brick wall and positioned themselves alongside the sentry who was manning the powerful Steiner binoculars, which the Americans had mounted on a specially designed bipod assembly.

"What have you got, Sergeant?" Sudden asked the soldier.

"Looks like a bunch of peasants, sir," Sergeant

Young responded in a southern drawl around a wad of chewing tobacco. The middle-aged sergeant had been on numerous missions with Oz and was well liked by his men. He scooted to one side, making room for the two officers to observe through the advanced optical system.

"They're armed," Young informed them, "but only with rifles, from the looks of it. A couple of the guns have pretty long barrels—black powder, I suspect. No machine guns or rockets, near as I can tell."

"Definitely not Chinese military," Sudden agreed, taking his turn gazing through the optics, which gathered enough light to make the distant men look like they were walking through dusk rather than darkness. "Take a look," he said to Oz.

The flier stared through the lenses at the men who were picking their way down the narrow path. "They're coming in pretty slowly—no night-vision gear, either."

"Do you think they know we're here?" Sudden asked.

"They might have seen us come in if they were on the ridge," Oz answered. "If they didn't, we're apt to give them quite a scare when they come into the ruins and discover us."

"But if they saw us landing, why would they be sneaking up on us like this?" Young asked.

"Maybe they think we're Chinese," Oz replied, straightening up.

Sudden swore under his breath.

"That could be it," Young agreed. "They wouldn't expect anyone else to be operating in this area."

"If that's right," Sudden said, "those guys have got a lot of guts, sneaking up to ambush their enemies in almost total darkness."

Young spit a wad of tobacco as if to punctuate the lieutenant's sentence. "Any suggestions as to how we're going to keep them from opening fire on us?"

"That's a good question," Oz said.

Young pulled a foil-wrapped plug of tobacco out of his pocket. "I have a sniper with an NV scope who could fire in front of them. Just close enough to let them know we meant business. They'll be in range in a few minutes if they continue at their present pace."

Oz shook his head. "Not yet. Let's save that for a last resort. I don't want to start shooting at the local friendlies unless we absolutely have to."

"Yeah, plus our shots might alert any Chinese troops that might be in the area," Sudden added.

*There is one other way,* Oz thought, *but it would really be risky.* "Have your sniper standing by and get your translator here on the double," he ordered Sudden.

"Forget the lower passageways," Major Ling bellowed at Lieutenant Woo. "Send reinforcements for the guards with the Buddha. That's where they're headed."

"Yes, sir."

"One of the monks—the only prisoner—says he is an informer."

"I'll speak to him later. We've got to stop the intruders first. Get with it!"

"Yes, sir." Woo saluted, spun on his heel so fast that he looked like a dancer, and jogged out of the room, yelling orders to the troops waiting outside the commander's bedroom.

*Bunch of idiots!* Ling thought as he threw the

quilted blanket off himself and swung his naked legs over the side of the bed, oblivious to the cold stone floor. *How in the world did the intruders get past the guards?* He could almost believe that the monks could make themselves invisible, as incompetent as his men had been lately.

He quickly slipped into his pants and slid on his boots without bothering to put on socks, even though he knew it meant the boots would be hard to remove later. Grabbing his coat and draping it over his shoulders, he headed for the door, pausing only to tear his submachine gun off the wall, where it hung by its strap.

As he strode into the hall, he racheted the charging handle of the Type 79 back and let it go, arming the weapon. No one was going to invade his fortress without paying dearly for it.

At the same moment the two soldiers behind Gompo fired, Targye let loose with his own volley. The blasts deafened him, prompting him to close his eyes involuntarily. But when he jerked them open again, one of the Chinese riflemen was falling. The monk forced himself to concentrate on the front sight of the rifle he shouldered. *You know how to shoot; use your skills,* he ordered himself.

Time seemed suspended as he gazed past the notch of the rear sight and aligned it and the front post on the remaining soldier, whose rifle muzzle seemed to flare silently, ejecting bullets the monk was convinced he could see coming toward him. The projectiles decelerated, passing his head as if time were sluggishly coming to a halt. Targye's finger squeezed the trigger of his weapon, and it spit silent fire; the bullet slid across the narrow distance between the two men, spattering against the chest of the Chinese trooper in a slow-motion explosion of blood and tissue.

The soldier stood for long seconds, his rifle sinking toward the floor, his face blanketed in horror. Then his eyes slid upward, the pupils vanishing below the upper lids as if losing the race with the rest of his body, which floated downward, finally flopping beside his companion like a limp rag.

Abruptly Targye's hearing was restored, and time resumed its normal pace. "Did it seem like everything was standing still?" he asked, glancing around for his companion. Had a miracle slowed down the passage of time? *And where was*— "Gompo! You're hurt."

The old monk was kneeling on the floor, holding his shoulder. The wound under his hand was leaking blood that soaked into his robe and dripped onto the stone floor, leaving flat red roses where each globule fell.

"How badly are you hurt?" Targye asked, knowing by the way the bloodstain was growing that Gompo was seriously injured.

"Never mind me—the Dalai Lama," the old man ordered. "We must free the Dalai Lama."

Reluctantly Targye stepped past Gompo and pushed against the heavy iron and wood door. *Locked.* "My *bodhisattva,* are you in there?" he called, peering through the iron grate on the door, his eyes failing to discern anything in the darkness beyond.

There was no answer. *Perhaps we have come to the wrong place,* he thought fearfully. They had never really known that the Dalai Lama would be in those cells. They had only speculated.

"Buddha, are you in there?" Gompo asked, shakily standing beside his worried partner.

"Yes," the voice came from inside the cell. "I have returned from my flight among the stars."

"Stand back, my *bodhisattva*," Targye warned, placing the muzzle of his rifle against the cast-iron lock.

"I am clear," the voice of the Dalai Lama declared from the other side of the heavy door.

Targye pointed the muzzle of the rifle at the lock and tightened his finger on the trigger, trying not to blink. As the massive explosion rattled the weapon, a jagged hole appeared in the lock, accompanied by a shower of sparks from the steel-jacketed bullet.

Gompo leaned against the door. "It's still holding. Let me see if the guard has a key—"

"He doesn't," the voice inside the cell informed them. "The officer in charge no longer trusts his men not to accidentally free me when my soul is wandering and they can no longer see my body."

"Stand back!" Targye warned Gompo, dismayed at how bloody the old man's robe had become. Quickly he fired the rifle four more times, creating a quartet of new holes in the lock and door.

As Gompo pushed weakly at the barrier, it swung free. "It's open!" he croaked, stumbling through the doorway. "Come, master, we must hurry if we are to escape."

The *bodhisattva* stepped forward into the light that emanated from the bare bulbs beyond the open door, shocking Targye with his appearance. The god looked much older and thinner than the monk had remembered; he might have been mistaken for a shrunken old man.

"This way," Targye directed his ailing god, escorting him into the hallway by the elbow the way a parent might guide a child who was unaware of the dangers surrounding him. "This way. We must hurry or the soldiers will have us all."

"No," the Dalai Lama said, refusing to follow his rescuers. "*This* way is the path we must take."

"That way is a dead end, master," Gompo said faintly. "I memorized the map, and it—"

"This way," the Buddha insisted.

Targye started to protest but held his tongue. It was not for him to question the ways of the Buddha. "Lead us, holy one," he said, raising an eyebrow and glancing toward Gompo, who nodded imperceptibly.

"But please hurry, master," Targye urged. "More of the Chinese soldiers will be here any moment."

The Dalai Lama strolled down the hallway, heading toward the passageway that Gompo had said was a dead end. Targye tried to remain calm, but he could hear more of the soldiers running up the stone stairwell behind them, and there was little doubt in his mind that the Tibetans would soon be cornered by the Chinese troops.

*Why is the Buddha doing this?* the monk asked himself. Did the *bodhisattva* want the three of them to be captured?

Or did he have something else in mind?

The Dalai Lama rounded a corner in the hallway in front of Targye and started down it, pausing for a moment as if unsure of himself. Then he turned around and placed his back toward the stone wall that cut off the end of the hallway.

*We are trapped,* Targye realized as Gompo collapsed onto the floor. For a few seconds he had hoped the Buddha knew a secret way out. But now his hopes were crushed, prompting him almost to doubt the god's divinity. The holy one's actions had seemed more those of a spoiled child than those of a leader of the world's Buddhist faithful.

In the hallway beyond the corner the heavy boots of a score of Chinese troops echoed across the stone floor as an officer issued heated orders. Targye listened fearfully; the booted feet came closer and the shadow of the approaching figures was thrown across the passageway by the bare bulbs in the ceiling.

The soldiers started to converse in Chinese, speaking too fast for the monk to follow their conversation.

Targye shouldered his rifle, raising it to cover the area ahead of him. *Why is my god doing nothing to protect us?* he wondered, his finger tightening on the trigger.

# 18

Private Joe Edwards trudged through the darkness alongside Oz, considering the two conflicting myths in existence about the Army pilot. One legend had it that he was crazy, and the other that he was superbrave.

*Now I'm not sure which side I believe,* the young soldier thought, fingering the Beretta M9 pistol strapped to his side. Somehow, going out in the night to talk to a bunch of wild-eyed tribesmen who believed that devils lurked at every bend in the mountain trail was an act to be totted up in the crazy column, especially given the wide array of weapons the tribesmen brandished as they crept through the night.

Edwards wondered how much his meager linguistic abilities might contribute to the apparent insanity into which he was heading. He recalled once again the old story that translators liked to tell to remind themselves of the potential disasters ill-chosen words could create.

During the late 1970s, as Jimmy Carter had addressed a foreign assembly, he'd told them, "I want to get to know all of you better." The presidential translator had used the native word for "to know" in the sexual sense, translating the American leader's message into "I want to have sexual relations with all of you." The meeting had gone downhill from there.

Private Edwards was acutely aware of how easy it would be to commit such a faux pas, given the limited amount of Tibetan he knew. *I'll just have to do my best and let the chips fall where they will,* he decided. He stumbled on the pathway behind the pilot, and a shower of stones slid off the trail, tumbling loudly down the hillside.

"Are you okay?" Oz whispered, glancing toward the approaching Tibetans on the trail far ahead of them.

Edwards mentally kicked himself. "Sorry, sir," he mumbled. "Guess I was thinking about what I'm going to say."

"Let's wing it if we get that far," Oz suggested. "Right now you need to stay sharp and not fall off the trail. Another mishap like that and either your neck will be broken or both our skins will whistle whenever the wind blows."

"Yes, sir. I'll watch where I'm walking." The young soldier silently swore at himself. If he kept it up, he'd probably be full of holes *and*—should he survive the barrage the rebels laid down—court-martialed as well. *Maybe the Army could shoot me, too,* he thought drearily.

The rebels didn't seem to have heard the falling rocks, and Captain Carson continued on toward the Tibetans, with Edwards tagging along.

*You're certainly getting what you asked for,* the translator chided himself as they made their way up the path. He'd joined the Delta Force hoping for adventure, but he'd already had enough of that to last a lifetime. He promised himself he'd jump for it if anyone offered him a nice, boring desk job for the rest of his tour of duty.

The captain paused in the middle of the trail. "We're getting pretty close to them," he said softly. "Let's get off the footpath here so we'll be to the side of them when they cross through. If the Tibetans start firing at us, we can hide in the boulders above the trail. If things *really* get bad, our sniper can distract them while we beat a hasty retreat back to camp."

Somehow that idea didn't reassure Edwards; he had never had anyone shoot at him from such close range. Sure, the Iraqis had shelled him a couple of times in 1991, but that had been impersonal—almost a game. He could see these guys' *faces*, they were getting so close.

*But at least we can see out here and they can't,* the soldier told himself, climbing up the steep boulder that overlooked the trail; the peasants on the path were stumbling along blindly in the darkness while at least he and Oz had NVGs. On the other hand, the monochrome green and white picture the night-vision goggles provided was far from perfect, and Edwards often had the claustrophobic sensation that he was viewing the world through an emerald-tinted keyhole.

The captain climbed the ridge ahead with sure-footed confidence, pausing at the top of the hill to take his AN/PRT-4 radio from its belt pouch. Thumbing the unit on, he spoke into it softly. "Sudden, we're in position above the trail where they'll be crossing. How's it look from down there?"

"We've got them covered," the black officer answered. "My sniper's got a clear shot if they try anything. And I can get my men to you in just a few minutes if we need to."

"Good," Oz said into the mouthpiece. "But don't have your sniper fire unless you're positive we're in grave danger. We'll probably spook these guys when we announce our presence."

"Yes, sir, I understand."

"Over and out." The pilot stuck the radio back into its pouch and turned toward his translator. "When you contact them, make it clear we've come to help them and that we are *not* the Chinese."

"Or mountain demons," Edwards added.

"They really believe in those?"

"Yes, sir; most of them still do. But Chinese is my best language—I just got a quick cram course in Tibetan before we left the States. It's not really a major language, and—"

"You better use your Tibetan," Oz advised. "If they think we're Chinese, I have no doubt they'll be shooting at us the minute you open your mouth."

"Yes, sir, I guess that would be right."

"Just do your best and we'll be in good shape. Now let's get down behind these boulders." The pilot motioned to a row of large rocks beside them. "After you establish contact, if they don't seem too antagonistic, we'll go down and talk one on one with their leader."

"Sounds good."

"I've been told I should bow, hands held out at the waist and my tongue sticking out. Is that for real, or did the briefers make some mistake?"

"They're right, sir," Edwards said, rubbing his nose where the NVG rested. "My grandfather on my mother's side traded with the Chinese—that's why I learned how to speak the language. He spent some time in Tibet, too. I remember him talking about how the greeting's done, although he was here about forty years back, before the Chinese gained full control."

"I doubt things change that fast around here," the pilot remarked. "Do you know *why* I'll be bowing and sticking out my tongue?"

"If your tongue isn't black, that means you're not a murderer. Empty hands show you don't carry a weapon."

"I've never stuck out my tongue before at someone to make a favorable impression," Oz said straight-faced. "But I guess that's the message I want to send. Get ready. They're almost here."

Edwards swallowed.

"Okay. Call down to them and try to convince them we aren't going to hurt them."

Edwards cleared his throat and hoped his meager Tibetan was recognizable and didn't have too much of a Chinese accent to it. He decided to start with an ancient greeting he'd heard from his grandfather; since the old man had said the Tibetans thought it was impossible for a demon to utter the phrase, perhaps using it would at least preclude the possibility that the Americans were mountain devils.

He cleared his throat again and yelled at the men on the trail below, his voice carrying over the rocks: "*Om . . . Mani . . . Padme . . . Hum*!" His stumbling diction echoed off the face of the cliff opposite them, and he felt that he'd failed with his first try.

He watched as the Tibetans on the path come to a sudden halt. They were silent for several seconds, then a call reverberated toward the Americans, repeating Edwards's phrase. "Hail to the Jewel in the Lotus. Come and join us in our fight. We go to attack the pagan Chinese."

"What did they say?" Oz asked, standing alongside the amateur translator.

"They're asking us to join them in their fight against the Chinese," Private Edwards whispered.

"Tell them we will come down but that we're Americans. We don't want to cause a panic when they realize we're strangers."

Edwards turned back and called to the Tibetans. "We are coming down. We will join you in your fight. But you must understand that we are Americans. Do not be alarmed."

A shocked silence greeted the Americans this time. Soon the murmur of frantic voices could be heard, the discussion muffled by the distance.

Finally the reply came back. "Come down. We will talk to you. But be sure you're not trying to trick us."

"What's the score?" Oz asked.

"A cautious answer, sir. They did ask us to come down, but they think we may be part of a subterfuge."

"Just so we can get down to convince them face to face. Once they see our uniforms and gear, they'll realize we're Americans—I hope. I'll lead the way. You ready for some adventure?"

The young soldier was startled and for a moment wondered if the flier had read his earlier thoughts. "Uh, yes, sir—uh, no, sir, no adventure. I'll be right behind you."

The pilot raised his radio to his mouth. "Sudden, we're going down to talk to them. This is it."


"They're demons," Bobolanga told those around him as he watched the dark shapes coming down the hillside. "That is why their words sound so strange to us." He raised his rifle, unaware of the sniper in the American camp who swung his rifle around to cover the old man.

"No, Uncle," Norbu said, reaching out and shoving the barrel down. "They are only men. But they may be Chinese."

"Why would they not just fire on us if they were Chinese?" Bobolanga asked suspiciously.

"I don't know. Let's wait and see."

"Perhaps the Chinese want to trick us and learn the location of the Buddha if he has escaped," one of the others suggested.

"Perhaps." Norbu nodded. But he didn't think that was the reason. "We must wait and see," he cautioned. "Everyone stay ready but don't shoot unless they start firing at us. Now be quiet; they're almost here."

The pebbles falling onto the trail announced the presence of the foreigners. Norbu strained his eyes, wishing he were an owl. *There.* The shadows blocked the stars above him. Two of them, he thought after studying the shadows carefully. There were only two. *They must be very brave or very stupid to walk down to meet a group of armed strangers like this.*

Were they really Americans? he wondered. It might be a stroke of luck if they were. But what would the Americans be doing in Tibet? More likely it was some kind of trick, he decided.

"Tranquillity to your house and the Roof of the World," the oddly accented voice called out. Norbu saw the two dark figures bow the traditional greeting, which he quickly returned. But in the darkness it was impossible for him to even see the strangers' tongues, let alone tell if they were black.

*I can't even tell if they have tongues!* he thought in exasperation. The situation was dangerous if not intolerable, he realized, watching as they approached on the trail in front of him.

"Those in the camp below know you are approaching," Edwards explained calmly. "They are Americans, not Chinese. So you can strike a light to see, if you wish. If you do so, you may—"

"Those in the camp aren't Chinese?" Norbu exclaimed incredulously. But the Tibetan spoke so quickly, Private Edwards could not follow.

"Uh, what did you say?" he queried. "If you could repeat more slowly," he suggested, his thick accent hard for the rebel leader to understand.

"How do *you* know the camp doesn't have Chinese in it?"

"You mean the men in the camp below us?"

"Yes!"

There was a flurry of talking between the two Americans.

"They talk in demon language," Bobolanga whispered to Norbu.

The rebel ignored his old uncle. Whatever they were conversing in, it wasn't Chinese or Tibetan. *That may be a good sign, provided it isn't demon talk,* he thought wryly. He'd better do something soon or his uncle would have everyone convinced they were mountain devils.

The dark figure spoke again. "Sir, those in the camp below are not Chinese but Americans. We were with them and came up the trail when we saw you approaching. We have come to rescue the Dalai Lama."

The men around Norbu began to mumble and

whisper about this last communication. Could it be that even the Americans had been called by the Buddha to fight the Chinese? It seemed too good to be true.

"Let us light a fire so we can see if the strangers are men or devils," Bobolanga suggested.

"We will light a torch so my people can see that you are men," Norbu told the visitors. "But we must get behind the rocks in case you don't tell the truth. We don't want to give ourselves away to those in the camp if they are really Chinese."

One of the strangers raised something to his mouth and spoke into it. The device crackled, and a tiny voice materialized out of the air. *Perhaps my arrogance has led us into a trap,* Norbu brooded. *Perhaps these aren't men at all.*

"We can step back behind this boulder," the one without the talking device suggested. "We can produce enough light for you to see us very well for a few minutes."

"We will follow you," Norbu said, fingering his rifle nervously.

The strangers stepped carefully over the rocks, never stumbling. *As if they can see in the darkness, like fiends,* the rebel thought with rising horror. But hadn't they spoken the ancient greeting? How could they be devils?

"We are going to light our torch now," the translator told Norbu after the two had come to a halt. "Do not be frightened, it is only a—" The man said a strange word Norbu did not understand.

"We are ready," the rebel lied, wondering if the light would reveal a pair of three-eyed demons ready to snatch the souls of the deceived Tibetans.

The shadow in front of him pulled a device from his belt and knelt down, laying the object on a flat stone. Then the stranger stood up and stepped back. "Do not be afraid; it will be bright," he said.

Suddenly the rock sputtered flame, and the night became brilliant white like day.

Those around the rebel leader gasped, first at the light, then at the strangers standing before them. The two were unlike any men Norbu had ever seen. They were dressed in strange helmets unlike those worn by the Chinese. Odd glass eyes glistened on top of the helmets like pairs of orbs looking upward, and marvelous weapons and instruments hung from their belts and pocketed vests.

But most of all Norbu's eyes fastened on the pale, corpselike skin of the strangers' faces and hands.

"They are demons!" Bobolanga whispered to the others, raising his weapon.

"No, Uncle," Norbu murmured, pushing the weapon down, then bowing stiffly at the waist. He stuck out his tongue and extended his hands to either side, returning the strangers' salute.

"Their tongues are not black, and they are not demons," the rebel leader asserted, a smile spreading across his face. He thought a moment, then chanted another ancient Tibetan greeting. "Victory to the gods!" he cried.

"Victory to the gods!" Edwards repeated.

"You see, they aren't demons at all," Norbu informed his fellow rebels. "They are Americans."

# 19

"The cell is empty," the guard reported to Lieutenant Woo.

"I can see that," the officer snapped. "Fan out. They've got to be close by; I can still smell the rifle powder in the air. They were here just a minute ago."

The squad of Chinese soldiers hesitated a moment, then turned away from the prison cells, running back down the hallway and the stairs beyond. Woo watched them leave, then turned back, once more inspecting the cubicle from which the prisoner had escaped.

*Is it possible that he's still inside but invisible?* the officer wondered, feeling foolish at even thinking such a thing. Entering the tiny cell, he stretched out his hands and felt around inside, trying to locate the unseen god who had been their prisoner. When he reached the end of the cell without feeling anything other than cold air and cobwebs, he cursed loudly.

*I'm as moronic as my men,* he told himself, disgusted that he would even think the prisoner could do anything out of the ordinary. *One stupid guard falls asleep and dreams the cell is empty and the rest*

*of us believe the holy man can work miracles! No
wonder Major Ling harbors such scorn for us,* he
lamented.

Woo stepped back into the hallway and inspected
the bodies of the fallen guards. It *was* amazing that
they could have been surprised and killed without
managing to hit any of their attackers with return fire.

*Perhaps the monks do have special powers,* he
reflected. But he reminded himself of the seventeen
dead and dying priests the informant had shot before
turning himself in to the guards. The monks were
just as frail and unremarkable as any of the other
Tibetans. They bled just like other mortals and now
were just as dead.

Woo's musings came to an end as he noticed the
pool of blood in front of the Buddha's cell and wondered how the blood had come to be there.

Checking the positions of the guards, he realized
it couldn't have come from either of them; there
would have been a crimson trail leading to their fallen
bodies, and there was no such line.

*Then one of the monks must have been
wounded during the fighting,* he deduced. And if
that was the case, there had to be a blood trail.
Searching the floor, his pupils narrowing, he spotted the reddish-black droplets that led in a barely
discernible pattern down the hall toward the dead-
end passageway that the crazed ancients had incor-
porated into the citadel's final stonework.

The trail of blood entered the cul-de-sac but
appeared not to leave it. Whoever had entered must
still be there!

The officer started to call to his men, then gulped
air like a beached fish, thinking better of alerting any-

one just yet. No, it was possible that one of the monks had simply gone there to die, perhaps even to distract the Chinese from the actual route the Buddha had taken. *Better check first and take him prisoner if he's still alive—that would impress Ling,* he decided.

Softly approaching the junction of the hallway, he unsnapped his holster and drew his Tokarev pistol. He first retracted the slide and then let it go. The mechanism clattered forward, noisily stripping a cartridge from the magazine and shoving it into the chamber.

Woo remained motionless for a second, holding his breath, and wondered if the noise would prompt the monk to attempt an escape. But nothing happened. *He's probably bled to death by now or is at least unconscious from loss of blood.*

Wielding the pistol in front of him, he slowly tiptoed to the corner leading to the dead end and peered around the edge of the alcove. Focusing on the figures in the passageway for only a split second, he was aware of rapid movement but unable to react before the butt of a rifle smashed him in the face. As he nearly regained his balance, a second blow bowled him over. Woo blinked, writhing in pain, and rolled onto his back, holding his face in his hands. He eyes teared so intensely, he could see only a flurry of red robes flashing past him before he lost consciousness.

Targye and the Dalai Lama rapidly retreated down the winding halls of the sprawling citadel, finally reaching its lower levels. The two monks ducked into one of the many recesses in the wall, hiding from the squad of Chinese soldiers that dashed past, running as if a mountain devil were pursuing them.

The priest grinned and shook his head; the Chinese seemed to be conducting a haphazard search, missing the hiding places in their haste to cover every inch of the huge complex. What had the westerner called it? A "Chinese fire drill." How stupid Targye had made them look.

Or perhaps the Buddha had blinded them. *Of course,* Targye thought, ashamed of his false pride. It wasn't his skill at all; it was simply the power of the *bodhisattva.*

*How childish I am,* Targye lamented, turning toward his charge. "Just a little farther, master," he whispered. With any luck they would soon be at the secret tunnel through which the monks had entered the fortress. The question was whether the Chinese had discovered it yet. "The way is clear for now," the young priest reassured the Buddha.

Leading the Dalai Lama down the dusty hall, the younger man was thankful the god had not demanded to choose their route. Being confined in the dead end had been like a nightmare. And yet the Buddha must have known it would work; the officer had inexplicably sent his guards away, then checked the hiding place himself. Two quick butt strokes had knocked him senseless. The monk smiled to himself for a moment, thinking of how the *bodhisattva* had outwitted the Chinese lieutenant.

Then Targye remembered Gompo and the others who had died in the rescue effort. It didn't seem possible that they were gone. His heart and mind refused to believe it.

Amdma. When he thought of the monk, he felt a flush creep up his neck. How he would like to smash the thin man's face! But he resisted even thinking about the traitor.

He must remember, however, that his fellow monks weren't really gone. They would be in nirvana or reincarnated as higher beings. He should rejoice at their sacrifice, death, and rebirth.

Yet he felt lonely and angry.

*Better keep track of what you're doing,* Targye warned himself, wiping a tear away with his hand and becoming aware of his surroundings. He wondered if they were still proceeding in the right direction, realizing he might have taken a wrong turn while he was lost in thought.

Up ahead he noticed one of the marks he'd discreetly carved into the wall with his knife to indicate the way back if anything happened to the map or to Gompo. Almost as if he had known all along he would be the only one on the return journey. *Think about these mysteries later; now it is time to escape,* he reminded himself. "This way," he whispered to the Buddha, his confidence about their direction restored.

The two rapidly crossed down into the depths of the dusty citadel, finally reaching the unlit corridor that led to the secret passage the monks had used to enter the fortress. Feeling blindly along the unlit wall, Targye's fingers brushed against one of the still-warm torches the monks had left behind. He knelt, setting aside his rifle, and took a flint and some iron out of the small pouch concealed in his robes. He hit the flint against the iron, sending a shower of sparks onto the oil-soaked rags of the torch. Bending, he blew the red ember into a flame that spread, lighting the hall with its flickering blaze.

The shuffling of booted feet reverberated down

the hallways close by. Targye lifted the torch and snatched up his rifle. "We must hurry, master," he urged. "They are coming this way."

The monks raced toward the exit in a flurry of ruby robes, the clank of Chinese equipment and the heavy footfall of combat boots warning them of the approaching soldiers.

"There they are!" cried one of the soldiers from behind the two priests, his voice echoing down the hall.

A moment later a bullet cracked past Targye. Running with renewed energy, heart thumping in his throat, he twisted around a corner and hurried down the branching corridor. Slackening his pace for only a moment, he turned around, fearful he'd find the *bodhisattva* injured.

"I'm all right, keep going," the god yelled at him. A second rifle blast filled the dusty corridor; the bullet ricocheted off the rock floor, singing shrilly as it passed.

Targye spied another of his notches and flung himself down the fork of the corridor. Twenty paces ahead of him was the pile of broken plaster and rubble left behind when Amdma had fallen through the barrier—a trick, the monk now realized as he slowed to a halt. "This is the entrance," he panted, standing aside so the *bodhisattva* could enter ahead of him.

"The hall of saints," the Buddha said, stepping inside the passageway to gaze down the line of mummified monks waiting patiently in their niches. The god seemed oblivious to the shouting soldiers racing toward them.

"*Bodhisattva*," Targye gasped, gently nudging the god forward to squeeze through the opening. "We must hurry." Backing past him, Targye was tempted to pull at the Dalai Lama's clothing to hasten him on his way. *What is wrong with him?* he fretted.

"One moment," the master said, reaching into the cobwebs beside the mantel of the opening that led to the hallway. "Do not worry—they aren't going to catch us here. Get on down the hall."

Targye's eyes grew wide with fear as he backed down the mummy-lined passageway. The scuffling of the Chinese boots coming from the entrance warned him that they were almost on top of the secret passageway. "Master, we must hurry if we're to escape," Targye pleaded. "Master, please!"

"A monk who resided here before the Chinese came once told me . . . " the Buddha began, his voice barely audible above the shouts of the Chinese. "Here it is." The god pulled at a half-hidden pin, stepping away from the opening. "Get back," he ordered as the board came free.

A groaning of ancient plaster and planks echoed through the halls as a large rock plummeted from the mantel, shaking the floor with its weight and setting Targye's teeth on edge with the high-pitched grating of stone rubbing against stone.

As one of the soldiers' faces appeared in the opening, a shower of broken plaster descended upon him.

Targye raised his rifle as the wall above the opening shuddered again, breaking apart and collapsing in a landslide of rock and plaster. The monk jumped back, wondering if the whole passageway was about to cave in. Cowering in the dust that blotted out the light, he dropped his rifle and grasped the torch, reassured that it could somehow protect him from the danger.

The rumbling ended as one final rock smashed to the floor, grating in the loose bits of sand and plaster.

Targye coughed in the dust and opened his eyes, holding his burning torch high in the mote-filled air in an effort to survey the damage.

"Don't worry," the Buddha reassured the younger monk, touching his arm. "The passage is sealed off from the Chinese. By the time they dig through, we will be long gone."

Targye nodded and rose to his feet, saying nothing. The air was quickly clearing, but the opening they had come through was now buried beneath a pile of rubble. For a moment he wondered if any of the Chinese troops had been crushed by the huge rocks. Then he recalled a critical fact. "Master, Amdma is a traitor. He knows—"

"Yes, I know Amdma is a traitor."

"If you knew—"

"Do not question the ways of the gods," the Buddha cautioned. "One day you will be fully enlightened; don't worry about Amdma now."

"But he knows where the outside entrance is to this passage. If the Chinese are quick, they can send a force outside the citadel and still cut off our escape."

The Dalai Lama looked startled. "Yes, that is true," he acknowledged. Then his face assumed its customary untroubled appearance. "If we hurry, we will escape. Now run as fast as you can. I will keep up."

"Yes, my *bodhisattva*." Targye turned and dashed down the passageway lined with the dead, the corpses now covered by a light layer of white plaster dust. The pent-up fear compelled the priest's sandaled feet to fly faster than ever before.

The torch he carried flickered in the stale air as he tore past the mummies, whose sightless eyes watched him and the king of the gods flee for their lives.

# 20

Oz, his flight crew, and Lieutenant Sudden Tomlin sat with the Tibetan rebels around the small Army stove, whose brightly burning Hexamine fuel tablets caused the rebels to marvel at the heat the unit produced. The tribesmen had quickly appropriated the device, and now they and the soldiers were sitting around it inside the shelter of the abandoned lamasery near Phuntsogling, where the Americans had set up their base camp.

Edwards told the Americans that the rebels insisted on another round of their strong tea, flavored with thick yak butter and salt. Since refusal of food offered to the soldiers would be considered a breach of etiquette, the U.S. troops found themselves compelled to partake of the exotic delicacy.

"Here, Captain," O.T. whispered to Oz, slipping a white antacid tablet into the pilot's hand.

"Thanks," Oz said. He sneaked the tablet into his mouth, hoping it would placate the rumblings in his stomach. The pilot forced a smile as the small cup in front of him was refilled with the strong tea. *I probably won't sleep for about four weeks with all this caffeine*, he thought. "Convey our appreciation," the airman instructed the translator, "and ask them to elaborate on where they were headed to see the Dalai Lama. Is it somewhere around here?"

"I think they'll tell us now," Private Edwards replied, warming his hands on a cup of the steaming brew. "We seem to have won their confidence with our gifts of chewing gum."

O.T. chuckled. "The soldier's universal friend maker."

The Tibetan across from Oz returned the Americans' smiles, nodding as if he understood the gist of what they'd said, if not the actual words.

The pilot reminded himself that while the people were poor and backward, they weren't stupid. He needed to be careful not to offend or slight them with any of his actions.

He took another bite of the excellent tortillalike *sanchuisanda* bread the rebels had offered and then turned his attention to Edwards, who was conversing with the leader of the rebels, a man known as Norbu. The swarthy man replied quickly to the translator's questions.

Edwards listened carefully, then turned to Oz. "They say they were going to meet the Dalai Lama on a plateau near Saga—a day's journey from here. It's called Janggo."

"But just a few hours' flight time," Death Song reminded everyone. "The position is marked on our maps."

"Then the Dalai Lama is free?" Oz queried Edwards.

"He's *supposed* to be, by tomorrow morning, sir. A bunch of monks apparently thought they'd discovered a secret way into the citadel where he was being held. They were mounting a rescue effort tonight, but it's anyone's guess whether they succeeded."

"Lucky we didn't go in, then," O.T. said. "If we'd tried to attack after the monks had gotten things riled up . . . " He didn't finish the thought, and everyone was silent as the possible consequences sank in.

"There's a chance the Dalai Lama might have been freed?" Luger finally asked.

"An outside chance, from the sound of it," Edwards nodded.

"They knew where he was being kept captive," Oz said. "That's a pretty good trick in itself. Perhaps they did have a way to go in and out without the Chinese soldiers finding out."

"But even if the monks were able to free their leader," Edwards declared, "it sounds like the big catch to the plan is that he has to travel through the pass leading to the Janggo plateau."

"Where the rebel forces are collecting?" Oz asked.

"Right." Edwards nodded.

"And you have to wonder how many people know about the rebels' operation," O.T. said.

"Yeah," Death Song agreed. "You start getting that many people in one spot and there're bound to be some loose lips."

"That's not necessarily true," Edwards asserted. "These people tend to be pretty close. Communities have clandestine rites and beliefs that remain secret for centuries. Sometimes the private ceremonies die with the people. If they wanted to keep something like this from the Chinese, they could do it."

*Then there's an outside chance the monks might*

*have succeeded,* Oz mused. And the Americans were just a short hop away from the location, since it was near the target of their aborted mission. "It seems crazy to come all this way and not offer a lift to the Buddha if they got him out," Oz finally said. "Ask Norbu if he'd like for us to take him to Janggo tonight."

As Edwards translated the pilot's question, the rebel leader became very animated, glancing toward the pilot as he answered and gesturing with his hands.

The translator turned back toward the airman with a grin. "This is a little hard to translate," he explained, pausing to think a moment. "Basically what he said was, 'You bet your toes and left testicle we want a ride.'"

"Tell him we'll see if we can't oblige," Oz said, rising to his feet and smiling at the Tibetans. "But be sure he knows it isn't a lead-pipe cinch just yet."

"Yes, sir."

"Death Song," the pilot said. "Let's get in touch with Commander Warner and see if we can talk him into letting us take a little detour on our way home so we can at least give these guys a ride to their meeting place and maybe, just maybe, give the Buddha a ride to safety."

"Yes, sir!"

"If that fool 'god' gets away, it will be my life when my superiors find out," Major Ling barked at Woo and the other four officers standing at attention before him as he paced up and down his room, sipping from cup of hot tea while the soldiers watched mutely.

"I promise you this," he threatened, his breath creating a fog in the icy chamber. "You will pay dearly *before* I do." He took a sip of tea, waiting for the words to sink in and was rewarded with the sight of two of his men growing visibly pale.

"I want you to take your squads and fan out over the mountainside," he instructed. "Don't bother coming back until I call for you or you've found that damned false deity."

"Sir," one of the officers ventured, "don't forget about the man who claims to be an informant."

Ling swore loudly and threw his cup across the room, where it shattered against the wall, leaving a wet stain. The major ground his teeth and then turned toward Woo. "Bring the monk you captured to me now. Don't leave until we find out what he knows."

"Sir," Woo said, snapping a salute and whirling to march out, visibly relieved at having an excuse to leave the tense gathering.

The major shook his head in dismay. Woo had seen one movie about the Nazis and persisted in clicking his heels sharply every time he saluted. "You." The major turned to the cowering private who served as the officer's aide. "Get me more tea at once."

"Yes, Major." The skinny soldier scuttled out the side door like a giant crab, hurrying to complete his errand. At the same instant Woo returned with Amdma, who was bound with cords that pinned his bare arms to his sides.

Ling stared at the man's face and then bellowed: "Free him! This is Amdma, the informant who gave us the Dalai Lama in the first place. Didn't any of you recognize him? Why is anyone going to want to work for us if we treat them like this?"

No one answered as Woo jerked his knife from its sheath, its blade telescoping from its green plastic handle. He turned toward his commander, eyebrow raised.

"Yes, cut them!" Ling ordered. "Do you have any idea where the Dalai Lama might be headed?" Ling asked Amdma impatiently as Woo quickly severed the ropes.

"If I'd been brought to you as I asked," Amdma said, turning to glare at the officer responsible for ordering him bound, "your men could have caught the Dalai Lama as he and the monks—"

"Monk," Woo corrected. "One of the monks I found died from a gunshot wound. There was only one other—"

"That you found and then let go with the Dalai Lama!" Ling shouted. "You were lucky they didn't cut your throat instead of just smashing your fat nose. Now let Amdma continue."

The informant rubbed his wrists as he spoke. "They've undoubtedly escaped from the entrance of the tunnel just outside Saga by now. But I know where they're headed; in fact, you can also destroy most of his supporters because they're rallying there to meet him."

"We could take care of all the troublemakers at once," Ling exulted, a rare smile flickering across his face. He pulled the coat draped over his shoulders tighter around himself and then took the cup of warm tea the private offered him, his anger seeming to evaporate into the cold air.

"Gentlemen, sit down. We need to plan quickly if we are to take advantage of our luck. Get me a map of the area to the west of us," he ordered the aide.

The officers sat stiffly around the table with their commander as the map was spread in front of them. Amdma pointed to the position where the Tibetan peasants and monks were waiting to join the Dalai Lama. "They are here, on the plain called Janggo."

Major Ling studied the chart in front of him a few seconds, taking a long sip of tea while the others maintained a deathly silence in the chilly room. Finally he pointed to the map. "If we hurry, we might be able to cut the Dalai Lama off here at the Tisangpo River before he reaches the pass leading to Janggo."

He took another sip of tea. "I'm also going to contact the air base at Yongden," he declared. "Perhaps they will scramble some fighter-bombers to head for the plateau. With any luck, they might catch the rebels out in the open and strafe them from the ridge with napalm.

"As for you," he said, looking at the officers around his table, "I want you to gather your best warriors from your squads and load them aboard three of our helicopters."

"Three?" Woo asked.

"Yes," Ling answered. "If there are more of the American helicopters still in this area, we don't want to leave the fortress without air support. Our remaining five choppers will stay here, with Lieutenant Woo in charge. And I want three of the S-70s in the air at all times. If the Americans catch them on the ground, they'll make short work of them."

"Yes, sir." Woo nodded.

"We'll transport our men in the three choppers to Janggo to retake or kill the Dalai Lama and then help mop up what's left of the rebels after the air strikes. I'll head this mission myself."

He stood abruptly, his chair scraping the floor and his men scrambling to attention. "Now get going; we don't have time to waste!" he bawled at them impatiently.

The soldiers scattered like leaves in a strong wind. Within minutes the orders had been passed down the chain of command, and the citadel became a beehive of activity, soldiers collecting gear and weapons for their pursuit of the Dalai Lama and his followers.

Within fifteen minutes the blades on the three Chinese S-70 helicopters echoed in the dark compound as the black fighting machines lifted into the air like giant bats, aligning themselves on their course in search of prey on the plain far away. Major Ling sat at the controls of the lead chopper, smiling serenely as he pushed the gunship through the star-filled sky.

# 21

"I'll give you a tentative okay," Warner's voice informed Oz over the pilot's radio headphones. "But try to avoid confronting any Chinese military forces directly until I get a go-ahead one way or the other from my superiors. I don't care to be wearing my tail in a sling because you get tangled up in another air battle when you're supposed to be pulling out."

"Yes, sir, I understand," the pilot replied. "We'll just see if we can give some of the Tibetans a lift—just a little out of our way."

"Right. And if you run into the Dalai Lama on the way, fine. But this won't be your official purpose, and I don't want you running a travel agency or spending much time searching for him."

"I understand, Commander."

"I'll be getting back in touch. Apprise me if you run into any problems. Over and out."

The pilot toggled off the radio with a tired smile, mentally reviewing what needed to be done. The fuel bladders were hidden in the old monastery so the two choppers could drop back by and refuel if necessary on their return trip from Janggo. At that point they'd pick up the injured, who were being left with the medic in the improvised base camp; this would keep the wounded out of harm's way if the choppers did run into any trouble.

*Most importantly,* the pilot thought, opening his side door, *I've got to empty my bladder.* He shook his head, thinking about all the Tibetan tea he'd drunk over the hour and twenty minutes since he'd met the rebel band.

Within fifteen minutes the air crews were in their MH-60Ks, the giant machines' engines thumping loudly in the frosty night air. Oz clicked the intercom switch on the control column and spoke. "O.T., are our dogs aboard yet?"

"Yes, sir," the warrant officer answered from the passenger compartment. "But we have some pretty wide-eyed natives, if you get my drift. I haven't shown them how to work the release on the shoulder harnesses, so no one can succumb to the temptation to jump off or climb the walls once we're in the air."

"Sounds like a good idea." Oz grinned, checking the control panel once again. The twin CRT displays seemed to glow brightly because of the light-gathering abilities of the NVGs he wore. Everything appeared normal.

He toggled his radio. "BC Five, are you ready to take off?"

"My Delta Force dogs are all aboard and buckled in," crackled the voice of Lieutenant Jackson, the pilot of the other chopper. "We're ready to roll whenever you are."

"Let's head up, then. Arm your weapons, hang on tight, and stay low."

"That's a roger."

Oz clicked off the radio and centered the control column in its neutral position, gripping the collective lever at his left. He throttled the MH-60K's twin engines until the rotor speed readout showed them at the correct RPM, raising the collective pitch lever. The chopper lifted smoothly into the thin mountain air.

"All right, everybody," the pilot said over the intercom, "arm your weapons. Death Song, give me the usual configuration."

"You've got it," the Native American replied.

The pilot carefully applied left pedal pressure to counter the torque of the engines, which tried to force the nose of the aircraft to swing to the right. His hover established, he then permitted the torque of the thundering engines to rotate the MH-60K around to their flight heading northward, increasing both the speed of the engines and the rate of ascent with the collective pitch lever.

As the aircraft climbed, its faint navigational lights blinked in the darkness; the pilot shoved the control column forward, and the helicopter nosed down, accelerating, its engines racing faster to make up for the loss of ground effect.

"Looks like we have the rotors balanced out," Oz reported, half surprised that a few wraps of tape on the titanium and composite blades could work such a miracle. "Now let's keep sharp," he warned the crew. The MH-60K skimmed the mountainside and climbed upward like a black banshee, with BC Five tagging behind it, the two helicopters blotting out the stars as they passed.

"Before anyone makes any cracks about me staying awake back here," Luger's voice called, "I want you to know I don't normally drink tea."

"Information noted and filed for future reference," Oz answered, pushing the control column forward and increasing the speed of the blades, bringing
the helicopter to its maximum speed of 290 kilometers per hour. "It just won't be the same without you
snoring over the intercom."

A gust of wind wailed across the shadowy peak
above them, bringing with it a flurry of sleet that
stung Targye's skin. The monk half turned on the
narrow trail to regard the figure behind him. "Are
you all right, master?"

"Yes, of course," the soft voice replied. "And
you?"

"Cold and tired."

"We will be there soon," the Buddha promised,
his robe flapping in the darkness like a shroud that
was barely distinguishable against the light-colored
rocks they crossed. "Ignore the sleet and wind. Soon
we will be where friends will share tea and warm
clothing with us. But we must continue on for now,
for the Chinese cannot be far behind."

Targye proceeded, the rifle he toted becoming a
heavy weight; he tried his best to forget the discom-
fort, but the frosty air tore at him, making his misery
impossible to ignore.

Perhaps he should try to disregard his skin and
concentrate on his other senses, relaxing as much as
possible all but his arm and leg muscles. *Ignore your
skin and fix your attention on trying to see,* he
resolved.

He strained to discern something in the darkness

but found only shades of blackness ahead of him; his sense of sight was not going to distract him, that was for sure. He decided to concentrate instead on the sounds around him: the pebbles crunching under his feet, each step making a different combination of pitches, the rhythm changing with the length of his strides; a small rat or mouse, frightened by their approach, sending a tiny avalanche of dirt and stones in its wake as it scampered out of their path; his labored breathing, rattling in his throat and combining with the cadence of his steps.

Then he heard another sound. Was it what he thought? He strained to hear it better. Yes, the soft roar of falling water. "Master, we must be nearing Tisangpo."

"Yes," the Dalai Lama answered from behind him. "We are almost there. Just a little farther."

Targye shifted his rifle to the other hand and increased his pace, gazing upward at the stars to determine the time. Nearly midnight, he reckoned by the positions of the twinkling points of icy light. It was late, and he was tired. And there was still the bridge.

The man and the god would have to cross the rickety bridge. Even in the daylight the monk hated crossing the shaky expanse of wire and wood that looked like it had been woven by an insane spider instead of by countless peasants. He shuddered to think of what the flimsy span would be like in the cold darkness.

But once across, it would be just a half hour's hike up the narrow trail to the Janggo plateau, where the rebels were waiting for the Buddha. Then he could rest and get warm. *Just a little farther and a little longer,* he promised himself, continuing the climb up the frigid slope, the howling wind whipping them with another gust and pelting them with bits of dirt and sleet. Targye struggled to maintain his pace. He was slowing imperceptibly when the tumult of rushing water abruptly grew much louder and the path leveled out. They were getting closer.

"Slow down," the *bodhisattva* warned from behind him.

Targye caught himself, abruptly coming to a halt. Unthinkingly, he had increased his pace when they'd reached the flat surface of the path; if he had continued on, he might easily have fallen over the bank and into the swiftly flowing Tisangpo River below to be swept away in the darkness, pounded to bits by the rocks that filled the shallow river.

He remained motionless a few seconds more, then continued on, slowly now, his free hand outstretched before him like a blind man.

"A little to the right, I think," the Buddha suggested from in back of him.

Targye turned slightly and brushed his hand against one of the steel cables that held the suspension bridge over the babbling river. Realizing how close he must have been to the edge before the Buddha's warning, he felt giddy despite the fact that he could see nothing but a black slash where stars seemed to shimmer in the depths of the Tisangpo.

"You need not be afraid now," the Dalai Lama comforted him. "I will go first; you follow me."

"Yes, master."

The *bodhisattva*'s robes brushed against Targye's cold skin like a ghost passing in the night. Then the monk could hear the steps of the Dalai Lama treading lightly over the planks, which were woven with wire and cane to form the swaying span. Targye stepped gingerly onto the bridge, wishing both hands were free. But he might need the rifle later; he must continue to carry it. His free hand gripped the teetering cable beside him; the steel wobbled in his hand as he followed the Buddha, feeling like a yak going to slaughter.

As they crossed the body of water, Targye tried not to think about where he was. But the swaying surface under his feet made such mental tricks impossible. The groaning and cracking of the planks underfoot caused sweat to break out on his face, even though the wind that blew off the water was so bitter that it seemed to cut to the bone.

"We're almost halfway," the *bodhisattva* tried to reassure him, his voice springing from the darkness up ahead. "The swaying is worst here—hold on tightly. But soon we will be safe on the other side. Everything will be all right. Keep that foremost in your thoughts."

Another board creaked below Targye's foot, and he released the rifle to grab at the cable, letting the gun slip. The fingers of both hands seemed to knit themselves into the wire and cane sides of the suspension bridge. *Perhaps if I wait just a moment to catch my breath,* he thought.

The water jabbered below him, and for a moment he could almost make out voices babbling in its depths. *Demons calling me to my doom.* He shuddered. He swallowed hard, realizing he had to press on or be frozen by his fear, unable to either advance or retreat.

As he inched forward imperceptibly, his toes scraped the stock of the rifle. Cautiously he bent to retrieve it, becoming aware of another sound as he did.

Was it his imagination? He froze in place, listening. Sweat broke out over his entire body, making him shiver almost uncontrollably.

The distant thumping was more distinct now, and he recognized the sound of helicopters, their rotors and engines muffled and distorted by the wind that blew across the face of the mountain.

"Master!" he called into the darkness. "The Chinese are coming."

# 22

"The six jet fighters are headed for Janggo right now?" Ling quizzed the air command over the radio as the S-70 slashed through the cold mountain air, searching for the escaped Dalai Lama and the monk who had rescued him.

"Their ETA is thirty minutes," the officer on the other end replied. "They carry payloads of our new Type 92 cluster bombs. Beijing is anxious to test the weapons in actual combat, and this is an ideal situation. You've become very popular with the Air Force, Major Ling."

"Good," Ling replied. "I'll have men on the ground with a radio to act as spotters by the time the fighters are ready to hit their targets."

"That would be very helpful," the officer agreed. "I'll inform the F-6 pilots."

"And I'll get back to air command with an on-the-ground evaluation of the weapons after the fighters have hit the target. Over and out."

"Major," the voice of one of the grenadiers in the gunner's compartment called over the intercom. "I see two figures on the suspension bridge over the river."

*Now wouldn't that would be a stroke of luck.* Ling grinned, altering his course slightly to direct them over the rickety overpass. He jerked back on the control column to reduce their speed and lowered the collective pitch lever, dropping them downward for a closer look.

"It certainly could be the two of them," Ling said, surveying the figures on the swaying bridge that spanned the valley of the Tisangpo. They wore dark robes, but whether they were red was impossible to say. He wished his NVG showed objects in color rather than green and white.

*But it certainly could be the two we're after,* he realized. "I'm taking us to the far side of the bridge for a closer look," he informed his crew. "Have five of our troops ready to cover that end. Then we'll drop back to the other side to block the monks' escape."

The pilot set his radio to the battle net frequency and toggled it on. "Two and Three, hold your positions on this side of the river," Ling ordered the helicopters following him. Dropping lower, he thundered past the bridge, violently tossing the flimsy structure to and fro in the wake of the blades, forcing the two figures to drop to their knees. *That should keep them from going anywhere,* he sneered.

The blades of the chopper created a flopping echo as he neared the cliff on the opposite side of the river and set down, raising a small tornado of dust. "Our soldiers are out and clear," one of the crewmen announced moments later.

Ling lifted the helicopter back into the air, turned, and retraced his path across the bridge, flying higher this time to avoid rocking the structure, since his soldiers were starting down it toward the two monks. He brought the S-70 into a hover. "Use our spotlight to illuminate the center of the bridge," he ordered his grenadiers.

The beam of light slashed through the darkness, impaling the figures on the center of the bridge. Ling raised his night-vision goggles and was pleased to note that the two figures wore red. *But are they the right monks?* he wondered.

He'd know soon enough.

Targye struggled to his feet, squinting in the brilliant light that cascaded onto the bridge. Ahead of him the green uniforms of Chinese troops shone as they cautiously advanced into the beam, their rifles held with bayonets forward.

The monk looked toward his feet, searching for the rifle he'd dropped. With horror, he saw it balanced on the edge of the walkway, teetering precariously on the pitching surface. He sprang toward the gun, and his fingertips grazed the wooden stock just as the weapon tumbled toward the water fifty yards below. Plunging into the inky liquid, it splashed inaudibly, the sound lost in the roar of the helicopter's rotors.

"Master," Targye shouted, clutching at the seesawing cables on either side of him. "I lost the rifle—we are defenseless."

"We are too exposed to fight them anyway," the Dalai Lama answered resignedly. "We must surrender. To do otherwise will only prolong our ordeal. They will simply take us back to Saga," he continued, "and we will escape another day. We will bend like the willow and spring back when the Chinese wind has stopped blowing."

Targye swallowed. He had heard about what the Chinese did to their prisoners, and he had no great desire to be captured. A willow tree might bend and sway, but he didn't think his bones would do so well. "Master, are you sure there is nothing else you can do to save us?"

"Trust me."

The monk looked beyond the Buddha; the soldiers continued to advance, rifles at the ready.

"Turn and go back," the lead soldier yelled, his spiked bayonet jabbing only inches from the Buddha's chest to accentuate his warning.

The Dalai Lama answered, bowing slightly. "We will do as you say." He turned to face Targye. "Retrace our steps," he ordered. "Do not be afraid. Nothing will happen to you until many long years after we've returned to Saga."

Targye swallowed hard, turned, and slowly crossed back to the cliff that overlooked the river, followed by the Buddha and the five Chinese soldiers.


Major Ling eased the helicopter forward, following the path his soldiers were pursuing as they forced their prisoners to the other side of the river. Skillfully, he kept the group of men centered in the spotlight to avoid losing them in the darkness.

When the soldiers had stepped onto the high riverbank, Ling's radio crackled to life. "It *is* the Dalai Lama," the squad leader informed him over the portable transmitter. "We have him! We have again captured the Buddha!"

"Hang on to the tricky bastard," Ling told him. "We're coming down to pick you up. Get both of them on board as soon as we land."

The Chinese officer set the helicopter thirty yards downwind from the soldiers and their captives. He watched the monks as the soldiers dragged them toward the helicopter, clothing flapping in the gale stirred by the rotors.

Within seconds his crewman called over the intercom. "They're aboard, sir, and the side doors are secured."

Ling lifted the helicopter into the air and toggled on the radio. "Two and Three," he called to the helicopters now hovering ahead of him, awaiting his commands. "You will proceed to Janggo and disperse your troops around the plateau. Once the fighter jets arrive, you will act as spotters for them, enabling them to wipe out the rebels there. Then you will transport our troops to the plateau, mop up any survivors, and assess the damage created by the new Chinese bombs.

"I'll be taking our prisoner back to the base," he continued. "I don't want to take any chances with him. You will contact me if you have any difficulties; otherwise, finish your assignment and return to Saga. Do not take any prisoners at Janggo. Is that understood?"

"Yes, sir. There will be no survivors after our combined attack."

Ling switched off the radio and kicked the pedals, directing the S-70 toward the citadel. The other choppers thundered past, dropping low to minimize the chance of detection as they approached the plateau.

"The Dalai Lama and the other monk are secured back here," the grenadier called from behind Ling.

"But the men are pretty cramped—there isn't much room with two additional passengers. Shall we bring a soldier forward to the gunner's compartment?"

The major thought a moment, a sinister smile spreading over his face. He raised the collective pitch lever, taking the S-70 into a steep climb, banking back toward the jagged rocks along the river. "With our informant back at the base, we have no need for the monk—we only need the Buddha. Toss the fool off the helicopter."

"Throw the monk off, sir?"

"Yes. See if his master has taught him to levitate."

The side door of the chopper slid open, flooding the interior of the aircraft with frosty air. Within seconds Ling felt an imperceptible rise in the chopper, as if it had encountered a sudden breeze. Twisting in his seat, he beheld the pirouetting body of Targye hurtling downward through the spotlight beam, finally vanishing into the darkness, his robes flapping wildly as he plunged toward the rocky surface far below.

*No, it doesn't look like he's learned to fly.* Ling grinned to himself, directing the helicopter back on course toward the citadel. The night had turned out pretty well after all.

# 23

The two MH-60K helicopters scaled the craggy mountain, hugging the surface with their terrain-following/terrain-avoidance radar, which guided the machines just feet above the jagged rocks.

"We've got some pingers over Janggo," Death Song warned. "They're high, with radar on, and they don't seem to be making any effort to avoid detection."

"Have they spotted us?" Oz asked.

"I doubt it—they just appeared over the ridge. I don't think there's any way they could pick us out of the clutter of these rock formations. But they're turning to go back over Janggo for a second pass."

"One, this is Five," the voice of Lieutenant Jackson crackled over the radio. "Our APR shows company."

"We've got them, too," Oz replied. "Looks like we're all heading for the same party. Hang on for a minute." The pilot toggled off his radio and glanced toward Death Song. "Can you tell what they are and how many?"

"Looks like four jets, two up front and two behind—standard Chinese attack pattern. Judging from their ping and speed, they're F-6 fighters. They're still on course—it doesn't look like they see us. They must be bombing the rebels."

"Pounding them," Oz corrected grimly, half to himself.

"Are we going to pull out?" Death Song asked, his voice indicating that he already knew the answer.

"Don't think so," the pilot replied, toggling on his radio. "Five, it looks like the four fighter jets are attacking the rebels. Let's see if we can even out the contest a little. Stick close—we're going in behind them while they're slowing to bank for their next run. Hang on and keep low."

"That's a roger, One. We'll follow you."

The two pilots guided the choppers in close to the rolling terrain, hugging the ground as they shadowed the four airplanes up ahead.

As the formation of jets ahead of them rose, for a terrible moment Oz feared they'd been detected. "We're approaching the plateau," Death Song alerted the pilot. "They're getting ready for their attack run."

Oz kept the control column shoved forward, pushing the aircraft to its maximum speed. He toggled on the radio. "Five, come up on the port and take the two on the left. We've got the two on the right."

"That's a roger, One. We're coming up now."

"Hit the rear plane first so they don't catch on. We'll jam their radio frequencies to prevent them from warning each other."

"Rear plane first," Jackson replied. "Activating EW."

Oz toggled off the radio. "Death Song, let's take out their radio."

"I've got it," the copilot replied, hitting a bank

of toggle switches that energized the electronic warfare assembly hanging on the strut alongside the MH-60K. The unit initiated powerful radio-frequency pulses on the bands used by the Chinese pilots up ahead; the interference was designed to make it appear the radios were malfunctioning, buying the Americans extra time before their prey discovered the actual problem.

"Hellfire is slaved to the target," Death Song announced, after lowering the monocle attached to his helmet over his right eye. The helicopters were nearly on top of the rear jets that now hung back as the pair of planes ahead of them readied for their first run at the plateau.

"Take them, Five," Oz ordered.

"Roger. Initiating our attack."

"The right rear jet is in my sights, Captain," Death Song declared.

"Fire."

Instantly the Hellfire missile lit up the sky beside the MH-60K, tearing away from the helicopter as a second burst of flame announced the launch of a sister projectile from the companion American chopper next to them. The two rockets illuminated the mountainside, quickly accelerating toward their targets.

"Acquiring the second target," Death Song said. "One is still on the mark."

Abruptly the night turned into day, precipitating the NVG Oz wore to block out all its light momentarily as its circuits cut off the signal, protecting themselves from damage. The image kicked back in as the flames ahead diminished, and Oz beheld a cloud of wreckage tumbling earthward, torn apart by the secondary explosions of its fuel tanks and bomblets.

The second jet, targeted by the sister MH-60K, exploded seconds later in another fiery explosion.

"What the hell are those guys carrying?" Jackson radioed to Oz.

"Looks like submunitions—cluster bombs," Oz answered. "Let's concentrate on taking them out for now."

"Roger."

"I've got the forward jet in my sights," Death Song announced.

"Fire, Two," Oz commanded. The chopper's second Hellfire tore away from its carrier, echoed by a similar blast from the chopper to the left. "Five, let's boogie out of here ASAP. I have a feeling somebody's spotting for these guys, and they might have some hand-held rockets."

"That's a roger—lead the way. Our second missile's already heading for its target."

"Breaking right," Oz warned, shoving the control column to starboard and sending the chopper into a banking turn away from the jets.

The Hellfires sought their targets and connected; another of the F-6 jets exploded, sending burning wreckage plummeting toward the ground below. The second Chinese aircraft, hit only marginally, lost its tail in the initial blast and tumbled earthward out of control. The pilot ejected from the spinning plane moments before it exploded on the ground, showering the valley with bomblets that burst into shrapnel and flames a moment later.

"Keep a sharp lookout," Oz warned both his crew and the pilot of the other chopper. "I have a feeling there're Chinese forces around here somewhere."

"Gremlins at five o'clock," Jackson called.

"What have you got, Five?"

"Two choppers coming up fast."

"I've got them on radar," Death Song announced. "They're coming at us at maximum speed."

"Five, let's spread out and get some elbow room. You head north, we'll go south."

"Roger, we're heading north."

Small-caliber machine gun bullets thumped against the skin of the MH-60K as Oz hauled it into a tight turn, banking hard to the right to follow the steep hill in front of them. Explosions erupted on the hillside, indicating that some type of munitions had been launched at the American chopper but had missed.

"What the hell are their door gunners firing?" Oz wondered aloud.

"They're still on our tail," Death Song warned. "The second one's after Five—we only have one on us. Hang on. They're climbing, going over the hill. They're off the screen now—behind the hill."

"They're trying to drop onto us," Oz said. "I think it's time for a little surprise." Pulling back on the control column, he reduced their speed as he kicked the right rudder pedal, pointing them toward the hill. He jerked the collective pitch lever, sending them skyward.

Abruptly the Chinese chopper topped the hill, pitting the two aircraft against each other, one on one. Bullets rattled off the MH-60K as Oz hit the fire button on his control column, sending a single rocket straight toward the S-70. The 70mm rocket crossed the distance between the two helicopters in the blink of an eye, smashing into the cabin of the machine and exploding.

The chopper seemed to shudder in the air, shrapnel from the explosion penetrating the gunner's compartment and cockpit, instantly killing the four crewmen inside. The S-70 hung in place a moment, then veered at a sharp angle, plunging toward the mountain below. It burst into flames as it fell, smashing into the rocks and scattering debris across the granite face.

The American pilot resumed his ascent, turning the helicopter north. "Let's see if we can help Five."

Before they'd traveled more than a few yards, however, they perceived the distant flash of a missile launch as the Hellfire from Buddha's Crown Five reached its target. The rocket smashed into the tail of the Chinese helicopter, sending a fiery blast through the interior of its fuel tank. The S-70 burst into flame, its cabin and rotors ripped apart by the explosion. As the fireball climbed, bits of metal and plastic rained toward the earth.

"Captain!" Luger cried. At the same moment, bright tracers arced past the MH-60K, announcing the presence of another jet. "From four o'clock," the gunner shouted.

Another salvo of projectiles passed; then the Chinese aircraft rocked the air with its transit, its engines burning brightly.

*Why didn't he use his missiles?* Oz wondered, kicking a rudder pedal to align them with the retreating jet. The answer suddenly dawned on him: The planes carried no missiles since they had expected no air resistance from the Tibetan rebels. They carried cluster bombs instead. Toggling on the radio, he contacted the other American helicopter. "Five, we have more company."

"Roger, One," returned the pilot of the other helicopter. "But no continuous-wave beams."

"Looks like they're only carrying bombs," Oz replied. "Just watch for their cannons."

"We've got one covered with a Hellfire. Rocket is away."

The jet Oz was pursuing was now in line. As he hit his fire button, three 70mm rockets hissed out of their tubes alongside him. The unguided missiles raced ahead of the helicopter, two slicing past the cockpit of the F-6. The third connected, climbing up the rear of the engine.

The blast ripped the Chinese aircraft apart, spewing its munitions into the air. Oz banked hard to the left to avoid the burning wreckage that shot toward them; within a split second the bomblets began detonating in the heat, propelling jagged shrapnel toward the blades and windscreen of the American chopper. The pilot swore as he pulled the aircraft farther from the tumbling rubble.

"Any damage back there, O.T.?" he called over the intercom.

"Only twelve airsick passengers," came the shaky reply. "A huge piece of metal came through my port and embedded itself next to Luger—another couple of inches and we'd have had two of him."

Oz turned the chopper and lifted it into the air, scanning the dark sky ahead of him for some sign of the enemy or his companion MH-60K. He toggled on the radio. "Five, how's it going?"

"Nice. Our Hellfire is off and—Hang on—Got him!"

Perceiving the flash of the American missile launch, Oz saw the projectile smack the oncoming Chinese jet headed toward Five. The missile detonated, transforming the aircraft into a fireball that tumbled toward Five. The chopper pilot banked away, secondary explosions of the plane's munitions creating a fireworks display around him.

"Five, are you okay?" Oz radioed.

"Roger," Jackson replied numbly. "Those munitions really come apart when they're hit. Damn, our board's lit up—looks like something hit our left weapons pod. Our guns and Hellfires are down."

"Stay low in case there are more bandits."

"Roger, One."

Oz yanked the collective pitch lever, taking them into the air for a better vantage point. "Keep sharp, guys, there may be some more Gremlins around," he warned his crew. Pushing his helicopter into a long banking turn, he circled the Janggo plateau. The sky seemed clear.

"Anybody got anything?" the pilot asked the crew.

"Negative on FLIR and radar," Death Song answered.

"Nothing on port," O.T. called.

"Ditto on starboard," Luger added.

Oz toggled on the radio. "Looks clear up here, Five. How are you doing down there?"

"Except for our weapons pods, we're in good shape," Jackson responded. "Don't see any bad guys."

"Let's drop onto the plateau and see if there're any rebels down there," Oz suggested. "I don't see any sign of them. Looks like the bombers made at least one run. Warn your passengers that some of the munitions on the ground may still be live," he continued. "Also, we don't want to stay down too long. I'm betting the Chinese will send in another pack of jets to toast us when they discover they've lost their jets and helicopters. I'll lead in."

"We're right behind you, One."

Targye had felt his heart would explode during the long plunge downward into the darkness. Nearly as bad as his overwhelming fear had been the sense that the Dalai Lama had failed to protect him and had been wrong that no harm would befall him once he surrendered to the Chinese.

But the fall had not killed him. He had struck the frigid water, miraculously landing in a spot deep enough to break his fall, and had nearly passed out before floundering to the rocks along the bank. Gasping for breath, he clawed his way up the incline, in shock from the long fall. He listened to the groaning of what he thought was an animal, then realized the noise was coming from his own throat. He shut his mouth, and the moaning stopped.

# 24

Oz circled the dark plateau, half expecting the rebels to mistake the American helicopters for Chinese and fire on them. But the agitated figures below were apparently too shocked by the cluster bomb attack to offer any resistance.

"Sudden," Oz called over the radio to Five, where the Delta Force lieutenant was connected via intercom. "You'd better have your men form a perimeter guard when we go in. But have the guards stay close in case we need to leave in a hurry."

"I'll have my men ready," Sudden promised.

"Death Song, Luger, and O.T.," Oz called to his own crew as he lowered the chopper toward the ground. "Stay with the helicopter in case we need to get it out of here in a hurry. Edwards?"

"Yes, sir," the voice of the translator replied over the intercom.

"You come with me. Have the Tibetans we brought with us fan out and see if they can find the Dalai Lama. I'll come with you to see how bad things are so I can report back to Commander Warner."

"You think the Dalai Lama could have survived

the Chinese attack?" Edwards asked.

"I don't know. There are a lot of casualties from the looks of things."

After the two helicopters set down and the Delta Force troops and Tibetan rebels had disembarked, Oz and his translator picked their way through a scene from hell, with the dead and dying lying in heaps on the cold rocks and dirt. The rebels worked to help each other, but the lack of medical know-how and supplies rendered their efforts futile.

"I wish we had some medics along," Oz muttered, but he'd opted to leave the men behind in the base camp with the seriously wounded.

"Captain Carson," one of the Delta Force soldiers cried.

Oz turned to see the American soldier accompanied by Norbu and a monk in tattered robes.

"I don't know what this guy's saying," the soldier said. "But he seems real agitated about something and insists on approaching you."

"It's okay," Oz told the guard. "We'll take it from here. Private Edwards?"

"Yes, sir," the translator answered. He turned and spoke to Norbu, who pointed to the monk and talked rapidly. Edwards asked a few questions, listened to the answers, then turned back to Oz. "This monk claims he was bringing the Dalai Lama here, but they were captured by the Chinese and carried off in a helicopter minutes before the jets attacked the plateau."

"You said this monk was taken by the Chinese?" Oz asked.

"Yeah, that's the weird part," Edwards said. "He says they threw him out of the helicopter and he landed in the river down there. Wait just a minute."

The translator turned back to the monk, who pointed toward the west and spoke heatedly.

Edwards swore under his breath and turned back to Oz. "Captain, this guy claims to know exactly where they'll be keeping the Dalai Lama once they get him back to the fortress in Saga. He's demanding we take him there and help free the Dalai Lama."

"This mission has been one royal pain in the ass," Warner remarked after hearing Oz's story. "So the sum total of armament you have is six rockets, one Hellfire, the machine guns on your chopper, and the rocket pod and side guns on Five?"

"Yes, sir," Oz replied. "The debris from the jet knocked out two of Five's pods, but we can transfer their Hellfire to our copter."

"Help the rebels on the ridge for ten more minutes, then transport the monk with you back to your forward supply base. Refuel there and await my orders. I'll let Washington know how things stand.

"*I'm* hoping they'll order you out at once," Warner continued. "But I'll be damned if I can guess what they'll do next. Things are a mess here between the Congress and the President. Several members are pressuring him to do more about China, unaware that you guys are already in Tibet." He paused a moment. "I'll get back to you as soon as I know anything. Over and out."

"What do you mean, you can't reach the choppers?" Ling demanded.

"They just aren't answering," the radioman huddled over the radio transmitter at the citadel responded. "There's nothing."

"Do you think the Americans are interfering?" Woo queried.

Ling rubbed his chin and thought a moment. "No. Our spotters at the mountain passes would see them if they came in. Our radar would pick up any jets. The problem must be that our helicopters are still on the plateau behind the mountains," he conjectured. "But I'm surprised they're taking so long. Our new cluster bombs must not be as efficient as the high command had hoped." He addressed the radioman again. "Keep trying every fifteen minutes and let me know when you reach them," he instructed.

"Yes, sir."

"I'll be in my suite," Ling added, stretching his tired muscles and clumping out of the room, Lieutenant Woo tagging along at his heels. "Have a firing squad ready tomorrow in the village square," he instructed his subordinate.

"Yes, sir. If I might ask?"

"The Dalai Lama. If he's dead, everyone will quit trying to rescue him. We'll tell my superiors he failed to cooperate and didn't appear susceptible to torture or drugs. We'll use the old American tactic of declaring a victory and moving on. Now leave me. I want to get some rest."

"Yes, sir."

*I should have tossed the Dalai Lama out of the helicopter or blasted him off the bridge,* Ling reflected, turning down the hallway toward his room. But a public execution would better serve his purposes, even though it would probably provoke a riot and force him to wipe out half the village.

Once word got out, however, that the Dalai Lama was dead, the monks would have to start a search for the new reincarnation of the Buddha. Best of all, it would be years before the baby they chose would be old enough to become a headache.

By then, Ling hoped someone other than himself would have to deal with the problem.

"I'm afraid I have bad news," Warner informed Oz over the COMSAT link. "President Crane wants you to complete your original mission with the men you have left. I tried to argue our people out of the idea, but they're afraid we won't be able to locate the Dalai Lama again. So getting him out of Chinese hands now, while we have a chance, is paramount."

"Yes, sir, I understand," Oz replied, sitting in the dark helicopter at the forward supply base they'd created in the abandoned monastery. "If we succeed, they're likely to be hot on our trail."

"That's for sure. Do you want to lay low for twenty-four hours and see if things cool off before you raid their stronghold?"

"Negative on that," the pilot responded. "Chances are they'll be moving him before long. And some of our wounded need skilled medical help right away. In fact, if it's all right with you, I'd like to send them out in our other chopper since half its weapons are gone anyway. We can transfer its ammunition and Hellfire to our chopper and carry all the Delta Forces that're fit for combat."

Warner didn't reply right away, and for a moment Oz thought he'd lost radio contact. Then the commander spoke. "Let's do that. It doesn't sound like the damaged chopper can offer much air support, and I don't want to lose any more men if we can avoid it. Strip the chopper of everything you can use, then send it on its way. In the meantime I'm going to have the fighters here standing by to back you up on your way out. Are you sure you don't want to wait until tomorrow after Five departs?"

"No, every minute here makes detection more likely, especially once the sun comes up."

"You're planning a daylight raid?"

"If we hurry, I think we can hit them just before dawn and head out into the sun so it will be hard for them to spot us visually from the ground."

"Damn, I wish we had time to get some more chopper teams in there with you," Warner said. "I thought Washington was going to scrub the mission—they nixed sending any Navy choppers in. They didn't want to risk more men, and now it's too late to send anyone in to help you."

"I know you've done everything you could to help us every step of the way," Oz reassured the commander.

"No condescending attitudes, please," Warner half scolded the pilot, sounding exceptionally tired.

"Sorry, sir."

"All right, I better let you go so you can get to work. Good luck on this one and call when you're headed out so I can get an escort to you at the border."

"Thanks. Over and out."

Oz shut down the transmitter and took a deep breath. There was some serious work to do if they were going to make the strike before dawn.

\* \* \*

After communicating with Targye through the translator, Oz realized there was no way to airlift the Delta Force into the citadel and expect them to reach the Dalai Lama before the Chinese could amass enough firepower to down the helicopter. The only way to free the Buddhist leader was to send a team of Delta troops in ahead of the chopper and escort him out into the open, where the helicopter could snatch them up before the Chinese could react with a concerted effort.

The catch was that the only way to sneak into the fortress was to scale the mountain face on the north side of the emplacement. And while the Delta Force was trained in rappelling, scaling a distance of that magnitude was pushing their abilities.

Oz turned to ask Targye another question.

"Sir, if I could make a suggestion," Private Edwards intervened before the pilot could speak.

"Fire away," Oz replied.

"If climbing the slope is a problem," Edwards began, "you've probably got people around us right here who are expert mountain climbers."

"That's true," Oz said, shaking his head as if to clear it. "Some of the best climbers in the world come from Tibet. I'm so tired, I can't even think straight."

"Everyone's bushed, sir."

"Okay." Oz nodded. "Explain to Targye what you're thinking and then let's ask around."

# 25

Four American soldiers, one Tibetan rebel, and one Buddhist priest scaled the granite face of the mountain on which the citadel rested, racing the sunrise that would reveal them to the Chinese guards who patrolled the area. The MH-60K helicopter, hidden in the rocks in the low hills beyond the village, awaited their call to come in.

The string of climbers spread vertically along the cliff, with Norbu at the top of the line and Sergeant Young, chewing a wad of tobacco, coming up right behind. Norbu gritted his teeth as the sergeant placed the gunlike device he carried squarely against the rock and fired a small piton into the granite.

Unlike the pitons and chocks Norbu had used on countless climbs before, these steel pins penetrated the rock instantly and almost soundlessly, anchored by the powerful blast of gas jetted from the automatic tool developed by the Army for such operations. The Tibetan placed a snap link into the piton, which was still warm from the friction of being fired into the granite. The soldier and rebel then hooked the lines tied to their harnesses to the ring and inched their way upward, finding finger- and toe-holds in the cracks and crevices.

"How's it going?" Sudden's voice asked over the radio Young wore on his helmet.

"Slow but sure," Young replied into the mouthpiece, trying not to look down. "I'd guess we'll be at the top in about ten more minutes."

"I don't want to rush you, but sunrise is coming in about eight minutes. Then you'll be hanging out there in plain sight."

"We'll go as fast as we can without falling on our butts," Young promised.

"Good luck. We'll be waiting to come in on your signal. Over and out."

Young glanced at the giddy drop below him, nearly a hundred yards straight down. *And here I am without my parachute,* he thought, spitting tobacco absentmindedly.

"Sarge!" came an angry whisper from below.

Young peered down. "Sorry."


Major Ling awoke suddenly, frightened by a dream. Rubbing his tired eyes, he lay back and took a deep breath. He'd dreamed that his helicopters were still out after attacking the Janggo plateau and that no one had bothered to inform him. He shook his head and closed his eyes.

*No, wait.* That was no dream. In fact, his radioman had never contacted him about the helicopters. Had the S-70s returned? He looked at his watch.

Six A.M.

*They should have reappeared by now!* Maybe they had and he'd slept through the thunderous sound of their approach. He closed his eyes, tempted to ignore his apprehension. *No, something serious could be wrong; you'd better get up and check on it.*

He threw the bedclothes off and rose stiffly, goose bumps covering his skin from the frosty air in the room. He swore an ancient curse as he dressed rapidly, promising himself he'd demote whoever was responsible for failing to report the status of the two helicopters.

*Can't even get a good night's sleep around this hellhole.*


Sergeant Young gritted his teeth and fired another piton into the hewn rock of the wall with the automatic piton hammer. Unlike the granite on the cliff below, here the penetration of the steel spike thumped audibly, magnified by the flat surface, and bits of rock broke away from the stone and rained down the cliff onto the men below.

*It's only a matter of time before someone comes to check on the racket we're making,* the soldier fretted, glancing downward. It was light enough to see all six of them on the wall now, even without night-vision gear. And there would be no hiding if a guard sounded the alarm; they were tied to the ropes, which were anchored to the stone wall. *Sitting ducks,* he thought, checking the sky as it grew lighter by the minute. If one of the enemy helicopters that circled the village from time to time came in close, it would spot them for sure now.

Norbu slapped another snap link into place, and the two men shuffled upward on their ropes, fol-

lowed by the remaining climbers down below. *At
least this little Tibetan guy's good,* Young thought,
gritting his teeth to fire another piton into the wall.
*Damn.* The automatic tool seemed noisier than
ever.

Norbu tugged at the soldier's sleeve and pointed
upward toward the edge of the wall six feet above.
The American looked up and saw nothing but clear
sky; then he heard the Chinese voices.

Even though he understood none of what they
were saying, he could hear the concern in their
singsong cadences, their voices growing louder as
they approached the precipice. Knowing instinctively
he didn't have time to unsling his carbine, Young
grasped the automatic piton hammer like a gun and
aimed upward toward the edge of the wall.

A face peered over the edge as Norbu flattened
himself against the surface, the snap links he carried
clanking loudly against the wall.

As another head and a rifle barrel appeared beside
the first Chinese soldier, the two troopers squinted
downward into the shadows, the red stars on their
hats catching the morning sunlight. When their eyes
had adjusted to the gloom, they perceived the phan-
tom forms hanging below them like giant bats seeking shelter from the daylight.

Before either of the Chinese troops could react,
two loud pops echoed down the ridge. Both men
slumped, falling out of sight of the men below.

Norbu stared upward, wondering what had happened. Then he glanced toward the American soldier
next to him.

Young held up the automatic piton hammer by
way of explanation. "Just like Roy Rogers, huh?" he

asked, blowing at the smoke curling from the end of the barrel. Even though he knew the Tibetan didn't understand English, he continued anyway. "Let's get a move on before their friends come looking for them."

The Tibetan nodded at this last remark, understanding what the soldier was suggesting even if he couldn't understand the exact words. He held the next ring ready while Young snapped another piton into the hard granite surface, grimacing at the noise created by the device.

When they finally reached the top of the wall, Sergeant Young was the first to scamper over the edge, ignoring the fog-shrouded panorama of mountains as well as the two corpses lying on their backs with pitons skewering their foreheads. Instead, he concentrated on watching for other guards along the walkway and checked the courtyard below, his silenced Colt carbine held at the ready.

Young glanced toward the wall as Norbu come over next, followed by Private Edwards and the red-robed monk who would guide them to the cells where the Dalai Lama was—Young hoped. The whole expedition into Tibet had gone poorly, and the young southerner wasn't so sure things were going to change now that they were in the heart of the Chinese stronghold. "Which way?" Young asked Edwards.

Edwards whispered to the monk, who muttered something back; then the private leaned toward Sergeant Young and pointed. "He says he thinks we need to go that way."

"Thinks?"

"Yes, Sarge. He says he's never been up here before."

"Great. Let's get going or we'll be spotted for sure."

When the last soldier had slunk over the wall, the group sprinted along the walkway behind Young, crouching to present a minimal silhouette against the sky. They crossed through the dark archway that led to a stairwell.

Sergeant Young stepped into the darkness and swallowed, checking the selector on his carbine to ascertain it had been slipped into its fire position. Then he cautiously started down the stairway beyond, squinting through the murk.

He'd hardly cleared the first few steps when a door on the landing below him opened and he spotted the green uniform of a Chinese soldier, who advanced up the stairs toward him, a cigarette hanging from his lips.

The man hummed to himself, sweeping the stairs with a broom. Only when he glanced up did he realize the American trooper stood above him. His mouth fell open, and his cigarette and broom dropped to the floor as he fought to grab the pistol holstered at his waist.

Young fired his carbine before the pistol was drawn, the heavy 9mm slug cracking from the silenced barrel, its low report echoing through the stairwell. The bullet stitched a bloody hole squarely through the soldier's chest; he tumbled backward down the steps, his heart ripped apart by the fragmenting bullet.

The American raced down the stairs, pausing to pull the body into the broom closet, wondering how long it would be before the Chinese realized three of their troops were now missing.

"What do you mean, you never got in touch with them!" Major Ling yelled, his eyes bulging with anger. "Didn't you even try?"

The radioman swallowed, wondering if he should lie or simply tell the truth and look death squarely in the eye. "Yes, sir. But you said to keep trying until I contacted them, and since they never answered, I—"

Ling screamed an oath, kicking the metal chair next to him across the room; then he turned and knocked the soldier onto the floor. The slight man stayed down, bracing himself for the boot he knew would be smashing into his abdomen.

Instead, Lieutenant Woo burst into the room.

"What?" Ling demanded, his foot poised for the kick.

"Sir," Woo said breathlessly. "Two of our guards are lying on the wall. We thought they were asleep, but they're dead."

"Dead?"

"Steel spikes stick out of their foreheads."

"Spikes?" *That sounded like the type of attack the monks would mount. Are they attempting another rescue?* Surely that must be it. The Americans would use silenced firearms if they were attacking. But the helicopters hadn't come back, either. Maybe the Americans— Either way, someone was after the Buddha. "Put the men on alert to watch for intruders and send a squad to support the pair already guarding the Dalai Lama."

"And you," Ling said, turning to the radioman.

"Keep our helicopters patrolling outside; have them watch the approaches to the citadel and the area around it. I hope those damned monks haven't found another way in here. And keep checking for word about the helicopters at Janggo. Check with air command and see if the jets that attacked the ridge returned to base."

"I'm sorry, sir," the radioman whined, "but you didn't give me a chance to tell you. The high command asked that you contact them as soon as possible because the jets didn't return last night."

Ling swore loudly, punching the radioman in the stomach, doubling him over.

# 26

Young fired a three-round burst at a Chinese soldier, who fell into a limp pile at the base of the stairwell. He stepped to the doorway and cautiously peered down the hallway. Observing no one, he turned toward Edwards. "Does the monk have any idea which way to go from here?"

The translator put the question to Targye.

"He recognizes this area by that faint X on the wall," Edwards reported. "He says the cells are a short distance ahead."

"Great," Young replied, spitting tobacco against the stone wall as he turned and cautiously advanced down the hall, his boots scraping lightly against the floor. As he neared an intersection of halls, he suddenly heard a party of Chinese soldiers running toward them, their loose gear clanking. Leaping into the hall directly in front of them, he unleashed his carbine, its stream of bullets pounding the six men and ricocheting along the walls.

Only one of the soldiers managed to return fire before falling, the bullet he discharged glancing off the wall beside Young's head. Young calmly dropped his empty magazine and shoved a new one home, his eyes on the dying men ahead of him. He hit the bolt release on the left side of the firearm's receiver, and the mechanism clattered shut, chambering a new round.

Edwards stood next to the sergeant with his rifle held at the ready, gaping at the mound of fallen soldiers. "Come on," Young ordered. "No time for sightseeing."

The Americans and Tibetans proceeded down the hall. Hearing the scuffing of boots as another squad of soldiers sprinted toward them, the sergeant turned and beckoned to his grenadier. "Valentine, get ready to plaster the end of the hall."

Private Valentine raced to stand alongside his commanding officer, lifting the M203 to his shoulder and sliding its safety off, with his finger resting inside the forward trigger guard. Abruptly the Chinese soldiers appeared, rounding the corner and plowing into each other as the lead soldiers spied the Americans and came to a halt.

Valentine fired at the mass of men, the 40mm projectile blooping from the launcher and smashing into the lead soldier, who was nearly blown apart by the blast. The other troopers, bowled over by the explosion, were quickly incapacitated by Young and Edwards.

"Cease fire," Young cried, seeing that all the soldiers were down. He approached Valentine, who chucked another of the large shells into the open chamber of the M203 and jerked the barrel on the slide, closing it.

"Lucas, keep a sharp lookout to the rear," the sergeant ordered the soldier trailing the group.

"We've created enough noise for them to know we're here. Let's get going." He turned to race down the hall, skirting the fallen Chinese on the floor.

"Turn left here!" Edwards directed from behind.

Young dashed around the corner and found himself facing two guards who were standing with their rifles ready.

The Chinese soldiers' firearms blazed, sending a wild spray of bullets careening down the hall. Young heard one of the projectiles smack into Edwards, who was standing alongside him.

Young ignored the barrage; trained at snap shooting, the American shouldered his carbine and pumped the trigger as he brought it up. His actions engulfed the two Chinese in a steady stream of deadly fire, drowning them with the fury of the onslaught.

Satisfied his foes were dead, the sergeant turned toward Edwards. "Bandage that," he ordered the ashen soldier, whose thigh was spurting blood. "You'll be all right, but we can't afford to have you pass out on us now. You're the only one that knows the lingo."

"Right, Sarge," the translator answered, forcing a smile. Quickly, he unsnapped the pouch on his vest that contained his battle dressing bandage and tore the plastic case open. All the while he listened to the monk who stood before one of the cubicles, calling for the Dalai Lama.

For a terrible moment Young thought all the cells were empty. Then a weak voice answered and Edwards started to translate the conversation, but there was no need; Young recognized the face that appeared behind the bars.

"Get that C4 up here and let's crack the lock on

this door," he instructed the soldier carrying the small explosive charges. Switching on his radio, he called the MH-60K. They had found the Dalai Lama.

Oz's headset crackled as Young communicated his message: "We've got him and are about in position for pickup."

"We're coming in," the pilot replied, signaling Death Song to commence the start-up of the idling helicopter. "Pick up position A?"

"Negative on that," Young replied. "I'll tell you when we get somewhere where you can reach us. This place is hot with Chinese troops."

"Keep us posted, then," Oz replied, hoping they'd be able to react fast enough to pick up the rescue party.

As Death Song activated the electronic warfare pod to shut down the Chinese radio transmissions in the area, the American helicopter rose like a giant dragonfly from its hiding place, rotating toward a heading that would take it directly to the fortress. Swinging his helicopter toward the complex, Oz pushed the control column forward, nosing it down as it sped toward its destination.

"Got a chopper coming in low at three o'clock," Luger warned over the intercom.

"Hellfire?" Death Song asked, glancing toward the pilot.

Oz hesitated before ordering the discharge of their last guided missile, but they had little choice. He shook his head in the affirmative. "Launch the Hellfire," he ordered.

Kicking the chopper around, he faced the oncoming S-70, whose guns blazed, spattering the

Americans with a hail of bullets.

"Locked on target," Death Song announced. The Hellfire jetted to life alongside the MH-60K. "Missile away."

The Chinese pilot didn't take evasive action; the missile flashed forward and crossed the distance, with the pilot apparently frozen at the controls. The S-70 exploded, lighting up like a second sun in the morning sky before tumbling to the earth.

Oz swung them back toward the citadel. Chinese soldiers along the parapet fired their rifles wildly at the approaching helicopter, but only a rare bullet actually connected with the MH-60K.

The flying machine lifted above the high granite wall of the citadel and dropped down toward the courtyard, discharging a rocket at the helicopter that rested in the center of the compound. The 70mm rocket left a smoky trail and connected with its target, crashing into the passenger compartment and erupting into the fuel tanks. A fireball climbed upward from the burning Chinese helicopter, the smoke from the fire swirling past the blades of the American aircraft, which hovered next to it.

Oz centered the control column to keep them hanging in their position. "Fire at the soldiers along the wall," he ordered his gunners, skillfully kicking a rudder pedal and slowly rotating the agile chopper in a complete circle. Flames from the Miniguns and the machine gun pod spit in all directions, ripping into the stone and the men who encircled them; empty brass spilled from the chutes below the helicopter, raining golden cylinders in the bright sunlight and bouncing on the pavement below.

Spying four soldiers lugging a machine gun into

place in a doorway, Oz discontinued firing his machine gun and nosed the helicopter down with a quick push on his control column; the rocket he fired leapt from the pod with a brief spurt of flame, chased toward its mark, then shattered with a blast that threw debris in all directions and crumpled the stone wall, pelting the helicopter with rubble.

Oz pulled the chopper back and continued his circling hover, firing a final salvo with his machine gun at a squad of soldiers that appeared below. They scattered before his withering onslaught, seeking shelter from the walls. Abruptly the machine gun pod exhausted its ammunition; the pilot swore and released the fire button.

As enemy bullets continued glancing off the underside of the cockpit, Death Song spoke. "I've got pings coming from the south," he reported. "It looks like helicopters."

"Sergeant Young, how're you doing in there?" Oz called.

"We can't get to the courtyard, Captain." The signal broke up momentarily, and then he continued. "We're going to try for the roof. Can you pick us up there?"

"You get there, we'll pick you up," Oz promised. *Or die trying*, he added to himself, lifting the helicopter to meet the aircraft Death Song had detected on the APR.

"I'll holler when we're almost there," Young returned. "It's going to be a few minutes."

"Be as quick as you can," Oz warned. "Things are getting pretty hot up here."

"Will do," Young replied.

A stream of tracers raced past the American chopper as it ascended, the pilot turning in the direction from which the enemy helicopters were approaching. He continued the rotation, whipping the helicopter to the side as another volley of machine gun fire was unleashed from the oncoming choppers. He glanced at the weapons stores display to double-check that he still had three rockets; his machine gun pod was exhausted. Looking back up, he centered the nose of the aircraft on the closest target and fired a 70mm rocket.

The projectile streaked forward at the same instant the Chinese chopper jogged to the left, clearing the missile's path. The rocket hissed past, crashing into the fortress beyond, raising a plume of stone and tile.

As the S-70 turned, its door grenadiers commenced firing, their automatic launchers plopping explosive projectiles toward the American helicopter. One of the projectiles connected with the EW pod on the struts at the side of the MH-60K, ripping the apparatus apart and showering the side of the chopper with shrapnel.

"What the hell was that?" Oz asked, fighting to regain the helicopter's balance. "Everybody okay back there, O.T.?"

"Some kind of grenade," O.T. yelled. "I think everybody's all right back here."

"The hit knocked out our EW circuits," Death Song announced.

Oz realigned the helicopter and nosed it down to launch a second rocket at the S-70, which continued to fire wildly with its side guns. The American missile crossed the space between the aircraft and connected with the side door of the enemy copter. The concussion of the warhead threw the door gunner standing at the grenade launcher into space; a moment later the fuel tanks at the rear of the passenger compartment exploded, ripping the machine apart.

Oz banked to the right to take on the second Chinese chopper, which recklessly charged toward the MH-60K through the flame and smoke, its machine guns blazing. The American pilot kicked his pedals, bringing the chopper around, and hit the fire button to release his final missile. The rocket coughed out of its tube and covered the distance between the charging helicopters, penetrated the Plexiglas nose of the Chinese aircraft, and detonated, instantly killing the crew. The out-of-control S-70 wheeled away, rolling sharply, and dropped toward the village below.

"All we have now are our side guns," Oz informed his crew after double-checking the stores display. "We're going to have to stay sharp to pull this off and get out in one piece."

As the radio hissed in his ears, Sergeant Young's voice carried over the airwaves: "Captain, we're coming up on the roof at the southwest corner."

"We're heading in for you," Oz called, throwing the MH-60K back toward the citadel.

"We've got another helicopter coming in from the north," Death Song warned. "About four minutes away."

Oz swore as he neared the red-tiled roof ahead and pulled the helicopter into a hover.

Kneeling at the corner of the dark attic, Young reached up with the stock of his carbine and smashed the butt into the tile above him. A shower of broken ceramic shards and dust rained down, bouncing off his helmet and cutting his cheek. Daylight streamed through the hole, accompanied by the thumping of helicopter rotors.

"Come on!" Young yelled to his men. Standing up so his head and chest were through the hole, he threw his weapon onto the roof and lifted himself out. Suddenly his boots slipped, and for a giddy moment he feared he was going to slide over the precipice to the ground four stories below. But his bare hands flat against the tile provided enough friction to check his fall. Carefully he scrambled to his feet and climbed to the peak of the roof, where the helicopter hung a few feet above the surface, the rotor downblast making it hard for him to keep his eyes open as he approached it.

Within seconds his men had quickly followed him up the slick tiles. "Get the Dalai Lama in first in case they have to leave us behind," the sergeant shouted to Private Edwards. The soldier turned to comply, helping the scrawny figure into the side door of the helicopter, where O.T. grabbed the Buddha's hand and helped him into a chair.

Norbu and Edwards clambered aboard, but before the last of the soldiers could climb into the helicopter, Sudden and his Delta Forces troops inside the passenger compartment commenced firing over Young's head, aiming at targets in the courtyard below. Young ducked his head as he boarded the chopper, return fire from the ground snapping past, the bullets thudding against the roof and side of the aircraft.

The sergeant flopped into one of the free seats,

strapping himself in as O.T. slid the side door closed and slapped the handle into the lock position. Then the warrant officer shouted over the intercom: "They're all aboard!" As the MH-60K nosed down, the few soldiers still standing inside the aircraft fought to keep their balance, dropping into the nearest available seats.

Young leaned back and closed his eyes, wondering if they would be able to outdistance the Chinese helicopter he'd seen rapidly overtaking them moments before.

# 27

"Land!" Major Ling screamed into his hand-held radio, motioning to the S-70 that was tailing the Americans. "I'll chase these dogs down myself."

As the helicopter came in for a landing, he switched channels and spoke to the radioman inside the citadel. "Get in touch with air command and tell them the Americans are making a run for the border. There are only a few passes they can get through, so our people can cut them off if they scramble some jets. If they can jam the American radio frequencies, that would be all the better."

"I'll contact them immediately," the radioman replied.

"Woo," Ling hollered, sprinting toward the helicopter settling onto the courtyard.

"Yes, sir," the lieutenant replied, tagging along-side.

"I'm leaving you in charge; I'm going to try to overtake these dogs."

"Yes, sir."

The major didn't say more, skirting the burning wreckage and broken bodies that littered the courtyard. He ducked his head in the rotor wash, jerked open the left side door of the cockpit, and half dragged the pilot out, ripping the man's helmet from his head and placing it on his own as he vaulted into the aircraft.

"Let's get these American devils," he hissed over the intercom, lifting the collective pitch lever. "Everyone out except the navigator and door gunners. I want to travel as light as we can." The doors of the S-70 were flung open, and the troops leapt out only moments before the aircraft lifted into the air. Ling kicked the pedals savagely, aligning the chopper with his prey.

"Sir," the navigator spoke, "air command reports that twenty F-6s have been scrambled to cover the passes between here and the Indian border. Military intelligence believes the Americans must be headed for the U.S. aircraft carrier in the Indian Ocean; the jets are being deployed to intercept the Americans. The military is also activating their EW transmitters to black out U.S. radio transmissions along the border."

The major shoved forward on the control column, a smile spreading over his face. "How soon will the jets be in position?"

"ETA is thirty minutes. That will cut it close if the Americans maintain their current speed."

"True. But with any luck we'll overtake them before the jets get into the area. That damaged pod still hanging on their wing strut will cut down on their air speed. And if they have as many men crammed in as reported, they'll be even slower—our chopper is nearly empty." He checked the gauges in front of him. "But even if we don't overtake them, our F-6s will cross the border to get the Dalai Lama—I know our leaders. The Americans will think they're safe, when in fact our jets will be going in for the kill. They'll make short work of a single American copter."

He pushed the S-70 to its maximum speed, smiling again as he anticipated the annihilation of the distant aircraft.

Twenty minutes after the American rescue of the Dalai Lama, the U.S. helicopter raced toward the sun that hung above the mountains, burning off the mists that shrouded the peaks and filled the valleys. Behind the MH-60K, the Chinese helicopter proceeded at top speed, slowly inching closer.

"They're still gaining on us," Death Song reported.

"This is just great," the pilot declared, fighting the control stick. "Something must have hit our blades and knocked some tape loose. They're starting to vibrate again."

"At least we're out of things that can go wrong," Death Song said darkly.

"Yeah," the pilot snorted bitterly, "everything's already gone wrong. Damn, I wish we could jettison that EW pod; it's really creating some air drag." He glanced out the side window at the unit hanging from its strut; the metal and plastic had been spread open like a blooming flower by the grenade hit.

*With our EW pod out, the Chinese chopper behind us can call in our exact position,* he thought grimly. Plus, if outside assistance came in the form of jets, he had no way to deal with it since they'd exhausted their missiles. "Is the radio still jammed?" he asked Death Song.

"Yep," the copilot answered, glancing at the display in front of him. "I don't know what they're using, but it's even knocking out our COMSAT frequency. I didn't know that was possible."

"It may be that our transmitter's damaged," Oz said. *Not that it makes much difference,* he added to himself. Either way they were on their own and probably dead men who just hadn't realized it yet.

A stream of bullets crossed below them, their green tracer trails barely visible against the sunlight as they arced toward the ground. "Looks like we're about in their range," the pilot said. He knew he could avoid the bullets by climbing, but the lower they stayed, the thicker the mountain air and the greater the speed they could acquire. Plus, staying low kept them off the radar.

"Better watch for the Ngamring-Tingri power lines," Death Song warned, double-checking the map on the horizontal situation display. "Looks like they're just three kilometers or so ahead of us."

The radar warning flashed and chirped an alarm. "APR shows more company coming our way," Death Song warned. "About five minutes off—looks like three jets."

"If we could just shake this damned chopper following us," Oz declared, "we might be able to lie low and lose the jets." He scanned the distance ahead and sighted the copper power cables gleaming in the sun, stretched between two massive towers on either side of the valley the Americans would cut through on their race for the Gangtok pass. "I see the power lines," the pilot reported. "How are we on flares?"

"Flares?" Death Song asked, surprised by the question. "We've got a nearly full store of flares. But I'd trade them all for one rocket."

"O.T., Luger, listen up," the pilot said. "I've got an idea."

"We've almost got them!" Ling gloated, lifting his helicopter slightly to discharge another salvo from the machine gun. He fired a long string that spattered off the tail of the MH-60K.

"Why doesn't our fire have an effect on them?" the copilot asked.

"The Americans armor their helicopters," Ling replied. "Our machine gun is too small a caliber to do any real damage. We're going to have to pull ahead so our grenadiers can hit them. Our grenades will create some serious damage," he added, surveying the broken EW pod still hanging on its strut on the American chopper.

"The Ngamring-Tingri power lines are coming up," the copilot warned.

"Yes, I can see them," Ling snapped, shoving hard against the control column in an effort to milk a little more speed from the straining engines of the aircraft.

"Grenadiers, stand by," he ordered. "I'm going to try to come alongside the Americans. Be ready; we may not have another chance to do the job ourselves. Our jets should be here soon, and we're almost to the border."

Ling watched the Americans dip below the heavy power cables stretched across the misty valley, the blades of the aircraft agitating the vapor.

Then the Americans abruptly slowed and climbed.

"What are they doing?" Ling screamed. "Fools!"

He yanked back on the control column, then checked his action, realizing that he couldn't ascend because of the cables stretched overhead. "Good trick—but not good enough," he muttered, maintaining his established course. The American chopper hung upwind, releasing a series of flares that blossomed to life and floated toward the Chinese helicopter approaching under them.

Ling fought the control column, trying to stay above and away from the miniature suns sputtering downward on their tiny parachutes. Although he didn't think they could damage the helicopter, he didn't want to risk getting the parachutes snagged in the rotors.

"Sir!"

"Shut up," he yelled, dodging the last of the flares. Glancing ahead, he perceived the cause of the copilot's concern. The MH-60K hung in front of him, its side door flashing open to expose the squad of Delta Force soldiers inside.

Before Ling could yank the S-70 to the side, the Americans opened fire with their small arms, the Minigun accompanying them. The windscreen in front of the Chinese pilot held, with only a few bullets whistling past, but its surface was pocked so badly that it was nearly impossible to see. The hail of hundreds of .22- and .30-caliber bullets threatened to overwhelm its protection.

The major kicked his pedal, trying to turn away from the barrage, which he recognized would soon overcome the thin plastic. He barely noticed the flame of the M203 grenade launcher fired by one of the American soldiers; the projectile smashed though the windscreen and exploded.

\* \* \*

"We got it!" O.T. cried over the intercom. "The pilot and copilot are both hit from the looks of it, and they're going down. It's a good thing, too," he added, "because both our Miniguns are out of ammo and most of the dogs are about out, too."

Oz didn't turn to watch the crash. He shoved the control column forward for maximum speed and prepared to dash for the border just a few miles away. "Any casualties on board?" he inquired.

"Negative," O.T. answered. "Everyone's okay, although the Dalai Lama is a little wide-eyed."

"Him and me both," Oz said, intently watching the area ahead as they charged down the steep incline. *There it is again, a damned jet.*

"Looks like we have company," the pilot announced, watching the F-6 glide in the distance, skipping over the mists of the valley like a rock on a pond. Moments later three other jets followed it up the pass, racing to cut off the American helicopter and keep it from reaching the sanctuary of Indian airspace. The American pilot swore under his breath, banking right while he tried to decide what to do next.

There wasn't time to set down or hide in the mountains, and the only ordnance the MH-60K carried now was a few rounds in the soldiers' small arms. He continued turning to the right, dropping as low as he could, wishing the Chinese pilots would somehow lose the American aircraft in the fog along the ground, although he knew it was hopeless.

"Their targeting radar's painting us," Death Song cautioned. "I've got at least two strobes at five and six o'clock."

"Stand by on the flares and activate the IR jammer," the pilot instructed, blinking at the wisp of fog that darted past the cockpit. The helicopter flashed along the ground, skimming so close that it looked as if the bottom of the helicopter might scrape the jagged rocks below.

"Jammer on and flares are ready."

"Missile launch!" O.T. hollered from the back. "Two—no, four."

*This is it*, Oz thought, waiting for shouted instructions from O.T. as to the heading of the missiles.

He continued to wait, wondering why O.T. wasn't telling him which way to dodge.

"Hang on a second!" O.T. yelled again.

The pilot continued on course, remaining quiet to hear O.T.'s instructions. *The missiles must be almost on top of us by now,* he realized tensely, awaiting the impact.

The windscreen in front of the pilot reflected a brilliant flash, suggesting that the warheads of the rockets had struck something other than the American helicopter.

*Their missiles must have hit the rocks,* Oz realized, the noise of the explosions echoing past the helicopter. "What the hell's happening back there, O.T.?" he demanded.

"You're not going to believe this, Captain," the warrant officer answered. "But the Chinese jets were just shot down. It looks like the missiles came in from behind them."

"Look at that!" Luger interrupted. "Coming up fast at five o'clock."

"What in the hell!" Oz muttered, turning in his seat to inspect the flicker of motion he'd noticed out of the corner of his eye. Suddenly his jaw dropped open.

Fifty yards away the pilot of an F-18 flew upside-down parallel to the helicopter, flashing the crew a thumbs-up from the cockpit. Then he accelerated ahead of the chopper, throwing his jet into a fast roll, showing off his skill in the fighter jet. The F-18 was joined by three other identical aircraft.

"So how'd they know to send in help?" Death Song asked.

"Warner must have realized we were in trouble when the Chinese jammed the radio," Oz answered.

"Looks like they want us to follow them back to the *America*," the copilot remarked.

"*That*," Oz sighed, "is no problem at all."

"The Dalai Lama has requested to see you," Commander Warner told Oz and the air crew several hours after they'd landed on the flight deck of the USS *America* and been debriefed.

"What's up, Commander?" Luger asked.

"He wants to thank you, near as I can tell," Warner replied. "He says he was slated to be executed and you guys pulled him out just minutes before the Chinese were set to ace him."

"Wow!" Luger whispered.

"We need to get cleaned up first, if that's okay," Oz requested.

"Just like a bunch of chopper jocks," Warner deadpanned. "God asks to see you, and you keep him waiting."

Duncan Long is internationally recognized as a firearms expert, and has had over twenty books published on that subject, as well as numerous magazine articles. In addition to his nonfiction writing, Long has written a science fiction novel, *Antigrav Unlimited*. He has an M.A. in music composition, and has worked as a rock musician; he has spent nine years teaching in public schools. Duncan Long lives in eastern Kansas with his wife and two children.